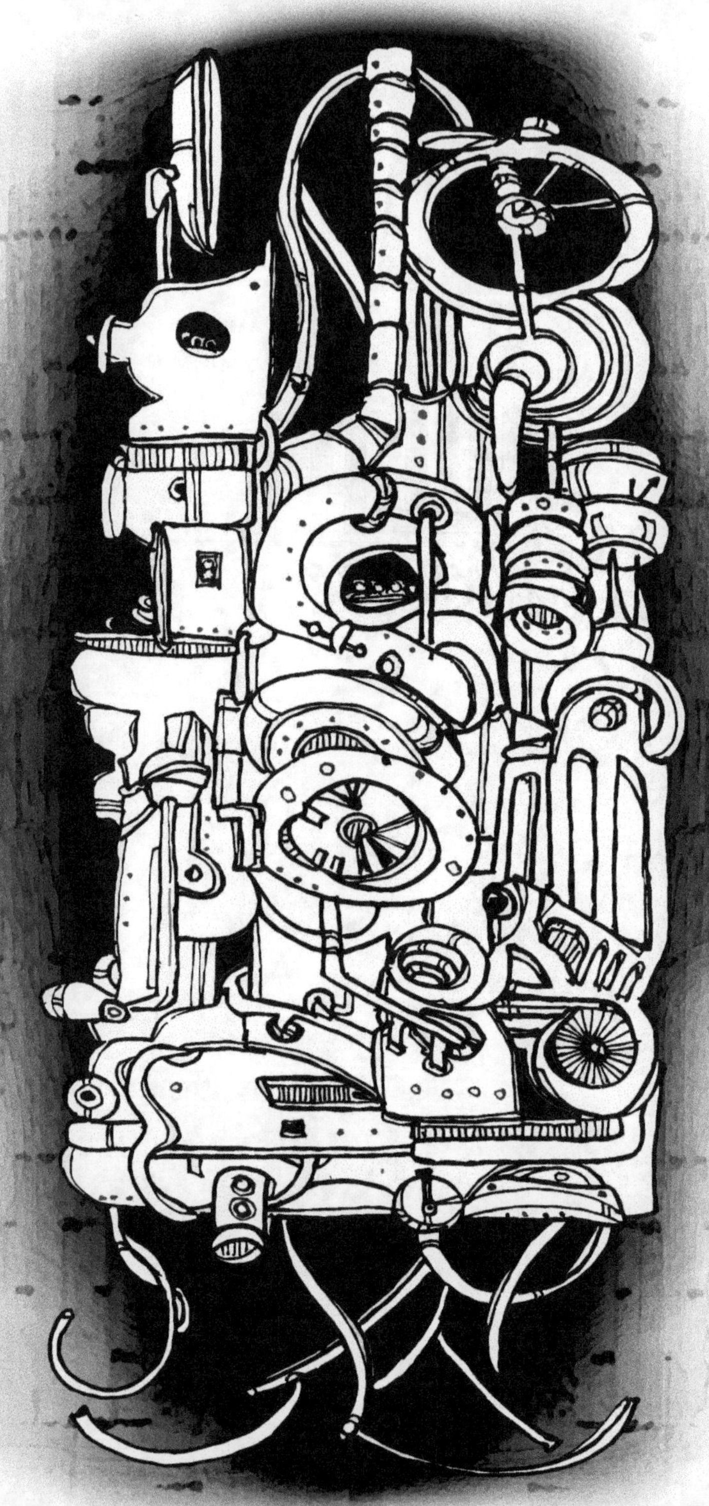

PULP LITERATURE PRESS

Issue No. 25, Winter 2020

Pulp Literature Press, Publisher; Jennifer Landels, Managing Editor; Melanie Anastasiou, Acquisitions Editor; Jessica Fabrizius, Story Editor; Genevieve Wynand, Assistant Editor; Samantha Olson, Assistant Editor; Daniel Cowper, Poetry Editor; Emily Osborne, Poetry Editor; Amanda Bidnall, Copy Editor and Graphic Designer; Mary Rykov, Proofreader; Kate Landels, Cover Design. For advertising rates, direct inquiries to info@pulpliterature.com.

Cover painting, *On Thin Ice* by Ann-Marie Brown. Artwork for 'Ghost Room' by Alison Bannister. Illustration for 'Treason's Fulcrum' by JM Landels and Mel Anastasiou. All other illustrations by Mel Anastasiou.

Pulp Literature: ISSN 2292-2164 (Print), ISSN 2292-2172 (Digital), Issue No. 25, Winter 2020.

Published quarterly by Pulp Literature Press, 21955 16 Ave, Langley, BC, Canada V2Z 1K5, pulpliterature.com, at $15.00 per copy. Annual subscription $50.00 in Canada, $68.00 in continental USA, $86.00 elsewhere. Printed in Victoria, BC, Canada, by First Choice Books / Victoria Bindery. Copyright © 2020 Pulp Literature Press. Written and visual art copyright © 2020 as per author and artist bylines.

Pulp Literature Press gratefully acknowledges the support of the Canada Council for the Arts.

Pulp Literature is a proud member of the Magazine Association of BC and Magazines Canada.

TABLE OF CONTENTS

FROM THE PULP LIT PULPIT

Issue 25. Twenty-five seems to be a big and important number. Young adults start dropping the 'young' at twenty-five. The silver anniversary is a significant milestone in a marriage, and a quarter is the smallest coin anyone honestly ever wants to deal with.

For a quarterly magazine, twenty-five is an achievement to be sure, and a milestone. But it's a quiet one. At just over six years old, the magazine has found a rhythm. Processes are in place, roles are defined, identity is established. As managing editor, I find I am able to take a gentler hold on the reins and trust the skills of our newer editors to build upon the framework Mel, Sue, and I have established.

Over the past two years, Jessica has taken on a large share of the editorial load, and last year we were delighted to have brought two new assistant editors, Genevieve Wynand and Sam Olson, into the fold. You'll be hearing more from them in the coming months while I take some time to work on my own projects.

But fear not, dear reader. The transition will be seamless from your side of the page, with the same great quality of top-notch stories, poetry, and artwork you've come to expect from *Pulp Literature*.

Cheers to the next twenty-five!

~ Jennifer Landels

*I*N THIS ISSUE

With the beautiful red pointe shoe of *On Thin Ice*, cover artist **Ann-Marie Brown** offers this issue's poignant opening act. Just as a dancer en pointe appears weightless, suspended in a moment of grace, so too do our authors, balancing the weight of beauty and sorrow.

Blood and booze set the stage in 'Wrap Party' as featured author **AM Dellamonica** takes us behind the scenes of community theatre.

It's turtles all the way down as **Frances Rowat** explores the itch and scratch of reckoning in 'The Smell of Antiseptic', and **Graham Robert Scott** and **Wallace Cleaves** consider the weight of legacy in 'A Parable of Things that Crawl and Fly'.

Two very different genies awake when **Susan Pieters** casts off ill-fitting confines in 'Buddha in a Bottle', and **Akem** explores capture and deliverance in 'Shotguns and Jinn'.

Elusive moments slip away as **Rebecca Ruth Gould**'s 'Hands' and **Allison Bannister**'s 'Ghost Room' remind us that love and memory are companion phantoms.

Adult children ask what is owed by a daughter to her mother, and a son to his father, as our Hummingbird contest winners, **Tatjana Mirkov-Popovicki** and **Chad V Broughman**, explore loss and longing in 'Afterlife' and 'Featherweight'.

Poets **David Troupes**, **Matthew Walsh**, and **Nicholas Alti** deftly guide us through landscape, dreamscape, and escape, each finding unique ache in the ties that bind.

And finally, two fan favourites reappear: **Mel Anastasiou**'s Frankie Ray arrives in Hollywood in part three of *The Extra*, and **JM Landels** gives us a prequel glimpse of Irdaign, her twin sister, and the caper gone wrong that sets the wheel of the Allaigna's Song trilogy in motion.

Happy reading!
Jen, Mel, Jes, Gen & Sam
Pulp Literature Press

WRAP PARTY

AM Dellamonica

AM Dellamonica's *first novel,* Indigo Springs, *won the Sunburst Award for Canadian Literature of the Fantastic. Their fourth won the 2016 Prix Aurora for Best Novel. They have published over forty short stories on Tor.com and elsewhere. Alyx teaches writing at two universities and is pursuing an MFA in creative writing at a third. Their sixth novel,* Gamechanger, *will be released in September under the name LX Beckett and is a hopetopia: a story that imagines humanity successfully navigating the twenty-first-century bottleneck.*

Wrap Party

"There's blood in my puddle!" A reasonable facsimile of Lauren Bacall, circa 1946, bursts through the Kit Kant Club door, stage left. Out of habit, she strikes a pose in the fizzing lemon light of the club's neon sign before confronting the survivors of the evening's bacchanal. "Who tainted it?"

Conversations stop. Heads lift off tables. Phyll, at the piano, croons the terminal note of a Nina Simone song into the sudden silence. Then a wave of drunken hyena yips drowns out all that jazz.

We found out about Lauren's puddle before we opened, when the props mistress mixed up a fresh tub of stage blood and dumped the old batch at the edge of the parking lot. It's a bowl-shaped pothole lined with quartz-flecked granite pebbles in an array of unremarkable browns. We're not talking the pearls of the Orient here. If they were paint chips, they'd have names like Beige Beach, Autumn Rust, Horse Chestnut.

But our Lauren — whose real name is Dani, not that anyone's checking the playbill — flipped out. Turns out she meditates there before every rehearsal or performance. When it rains, the pool formed is pretty enough. The water shines clear when it's not full of stage blood. The surface mirrors the clouds, and the pebbles glint back flecks of sunshine. Lauren appreciates a good visual.

Anyway, she *tends* the thing: keeps the cigarette butts, drowned wasps, and twigs from accumulating. When the rain dries up, she fills the puddle herself.

"Jeezis, Lauren, OCD much?" says a musician.

"All hail the sacred pothole." Phyll has been sitting at the piano, away from the others, drinking and playing, playing and drinking. She takes up her glass and toasts me. I return the gesture then pour another shot of tap water from a too-pricey-to-share bottle of boutique gin. I even dress it up with fizz and a twist of lime. The only thing worse than being the sober one among a crowd of the blind is the blowback when they realize you're a bonafide, full-bore stick in the mud.

"Where's the props mistress?" Lauren demands.

"Rosey went home."

"Allllll the grownups went home," drawls one of the jazz kids, waving his saxophone.

The company is split between two age cohorts. The back-stage folk—the director, my fellow designers, the department heads—have mostly passed that magical threshold, after which you take three different kinds of vitamins twice a day and com-mence with the yoga even if you hate exercise. They've gotten far enough financially that they can shell out to go to Europe, but they throw away three vacation days at the end of every trip to come back early, see the chiropractor, sleep off the jet lag, rebalance the chi, that sort of thing.

The actors and jazz band, meanwhile, are new-fledged, just

paroled from twenty hard years of helicopter parenting. They've *heard* the world has edges, but nothing's ever sliced into them. The idea of harsh realities feels as suspect as Mommy's tales of Santa Claus. Fuzzy on the difference between hardship and hangover, they're still partying.

In the middle, agewise, it's just me and Phyll. Beautiful, hard-bitten Phyll, our lady Marlowe, our star. She runs her big graceful hand over the keyboard again, making a caress of it. She knows full well I'm staring.

I yank my attention elsewhere. "Rosey's not mucking out blood bottles tonight, Lauren. She had a beer and went home to tuck in her kids."

Lauren smoothes her sexy-dame cocktail dress, wobbling on three inch heels. Her forties hairdo holds rock-steady. Lots of hairspray, I guess. "I am telling you now, Sammy, there's blood in my hole."

Screams of laughter from the boys at the unfortunate phrasing.

In the normal course of things, blood-dumping and set demolition *would* have happened tonight, after curtain and before the drinking began. But the cast assembled their own costumes for this show; they'll wear them home. The prop guns are locked in the stage manager's office. And we borrowed the neon sign and bandstand, so Theatre Passet is coming by tomorrow, with a truck, to reclaim them.

The backdrops for the set, though, they're mine.

I painted the murals first, then made photographs of the walls. We project them onto a silk scrim, switching from scene to scene with a bounce of a fingertip against a touch screen.

Cue one: the back alley of Saint Nicholas Hospital, dotted with working girls and johns.

Cue two: the swanky avenue where Lauren's character lives in cat-on-a-cushion comfort under the watchful eye of a mob boss boyfriend. In the foreground, a big car with fins, tinted in Neptune Blue. In the background, trees, their shadowy trunks abundant with leaves shaded Espalier, Lacewing, and Vegan. Old oaks for old money, trees that predate the First World War.

Cue three: slow dissolve to venetian window blinds—this play's noir, so you gotta have window blinds—half-pulled to reveal the interior of the office of Phyllis Marlow, Pee Eye.

Cue four: Glossy stills of a young actress, painted in an array of greys. Cathedral Grey, Cotton Grey, and Morning Mist, mostly. For highlights, we have reds. Flamingo Tinge, Vesuvius Flow, Spice Market, Crimson Glory. I guess your average homeowner isn't going to buy a shade tagged Sunrise at the Abattoir.

Crumpled bits of litter, battered antique doors, a couple gang tags and a nineteen-seventies portrait of Queen Elizabeth under-lie the images, adding a touch of disturbing surrealism. So I like to think, anyway. Using a scrim is cheap and flexible, and my hope was to make it all look like the actors were walking around inside a graphic novel.

Did it work? Dunno. The reviewers were too taken with Phyll, as usual, to make much note of the frosting. I can't fault 'em for that.

Onstage, Lauren seems to realize there's no sympathy forth-coming for the fouling of her meditation pool. She lets out a frustrated yip and totters out. The boys applaud.

"Leave her alone, you guys." That's our other ingénue, little Mackenzie Day, a gossipy method actor with a thing for collecting other people's traumas. She's built like a china doll, like the doomed girl in cue four, Susanna Sabine.

The play, *Cutting Room*, is a loose assemblage of scenes based on Susanna's unsolved murder here in the Saint Nick district. The Sable Starlet, they call her. The story resurfaces in the media every few years, when real news is in drought.

Susanna was like one of Lauren's puddle pebbles: sparkly enough in her way, but one of a hundred. She'd finished a run in *Othello*, right here in this venerable theatre. On closing night, sometime after the wrap party, she found out she hadn't got some big movie role that was supposed to catapult her all the way to Hollywood.

Some say it was a wake-up call; others, a last straw. Whichever cliché you favour, Susanna broke up with her married boyfriend, got engaged to her stand-up fella, and told her co-stars she was going to apply to nursing college. Stories have it she left a vaguely worded message for a reporter at the local crime desk.

They found her at dawn, in the arms of the Saint Nicholas statue at the hospital. Her throat and wrists had been unzipped—probably by a straight razor—and her body was covered in a black sable coat. Nobody's learned whose coat, though her fans on the Internet have plenty of theories. My baby sister's *Solve Susanna* site is currently masticating the idea it came off the police commissioner's girlfriend.

When the theatre company was spitballing ideas for this show, they found a pile of Sable Starlet clippings lying around the green room. You might say they got inspired.

Cutting Room has a corrupt cop and his pure-hearted constable sidekick. It has gangsters, shady doctors, a crusading reporter, and a sexy film star—that'd be Lauren—with a violent Lothario boyfriend. Principal roles went to Phyll, Lauren, Mackenzie, and two fellows named Burt and Mitch. The jazz band did double duty in incidental roles, playing suspects, witnesses, journalists, nuns, winos, and street perverts.

Phyll abandons the piano, gliding over to clink her latest shot of whiskey against my undercover gin bottle. "You usually clear out before we can get all undignified, Sammy." Her diction is clearer than that of the others, though she's drunk twice as much as any of them. Possibly twice as much as *all* of them. "You sheepdogging the wrap party for a reason?"

Because you'll drive home if I give you half a chance. What I say, pushing the words past a clenched jaw, is, "Keeping an eye on the girls and their glasses."

"Why?" Phyll was made—self-made—to play prime ministers and generals, queens and goddesses. Lucretia Borgia, Maggie Thatcher, Laura Secord, Catherine of Aragon types. People still choke up over her *Saint Joan*, and that was ten years back.

She's not beautiful in the conventional sense. Her eyes are mud brown, her hair a wind-thrown toss of prairie straw. She's broad-shouldered, thick in the trunk, and her jaw's square. Mannish, the reviewers sometimes say. She is, in every way, the antithesis of the standard pixie actress.

But put her in a properly cut dress, and you see her figure, draped properly, is a va-va-voom hourglass.

And, curves aside, she's mesmerizing. Give her a mic and a crowd, and she can twist them any which way you want: whip them up, calm 'em down. Bust their guts laughing, then rock them to sleep. There's always someone running after Phyll, begging for her attention, hot as a kid after an ice cream truck.

Onstage, if Phyll whispers, everyone in the audience leans forward. Everyone. Every time. You know how rare that is? Every time, I swear. Nobody breathes until she lets them.

At the end of act one of this show, when she finds Mackenzie's body, it's the look on her face that makes people flinch, gasp, cover their mouths, even start to cry.

When she stands this close to me, I feel air molecules racing between us, driven like mad wasps, generating heat dense enough to melt my clothes off.

I cool things off, as always, by breaking out the bad Bogey impression I used to use on my sister: "Little boid tells me Mitch might have designs on one of the goils."

Mitch would be our square-jawed Gary Cooper type, cast as a straight-up constable who also happened to be Susanna Sabine's *unmarried* boyfriend.

"Date rape?" Phyll is unconvinced. "Far's I can tell, either or both of our ingénues would bone Mitch sober."

"They aren't sober, are they?" That pissy edge comes out in my voice. Watching people get stupid makes me angry. I shouldn't judge, I know. Yet —

"Sammy."

"Someone" — the person in question is the hippie drug dealer who reigns in the ruins of Saint Nick's hospital, medicating the homeless, but I leave Sacker and our long association out of the story — "said Mitch was trying to buy Rohypnol."

"Mitch isn't that kind of kid."

"Something's up with him lately. He's been out of it."

"He's no predator. He's a Care Bear."

"Yeah. But what else do you do with that shit?"

"Care Bear can't dose their drinks if he's not even here," she points out. It's true: Mitch is AWOL. Some mother hen I am.

By now, we've all forgotten Lauren. Everyone jumps when we hear her voice, echoing backstage: "Where's that garden hose?"

"Ohmigod, she's gonna clean her puddle." Our trombone player laughs so hard that red wine drizzles from his nose. The kids rise as one, a pack of drunken puppies on the hunt.

"I'll see if Mitch is in the dressing room," Phyll murmurs, heading backstage. I have a brief vision of her and me as the grown-up dogs in that Disney thing about the stolen Dalmatians.

"Thanks."

Mackenzie gloms onto me as I go in pursuit of the cast. Her wrists are tinted red with residue from the stage blood. *Candy Apple Massacre*, I think. Where's the fun of seeing in paint colours if you can't make up your own?

"I know what you're up to," she says, dragging me off balance as she fails to walk a straight line. "I tried your so-called gin."

Dammit. "I'm allergic to booze, Mackenzie."

"Were your parents alcoholics?"

"Yeah, my dad drank," I say. The truth comes out glib, and I see her discard it. In my voice she hears wiseass faux agreement, not nights spent holding my terrified four-year-old-sister over the kitchen sink.

Pee, goddammit, baby, pee already.

I can't, Sammy, I can't, you'll drop me.

I won't, you won't fall, please just pee.

All in whispers, because God save us if we wake Dad when he's passed out on the toilet.

Stuka parenting, I think.

Mackenzie elbows me as if we're in on a conspiracy. She thinks she'll get other chances to play 'quiz the teetotaller'. She's forgotten the show is a wrap.

A bottleneck at the backstage door turns into a mass stumble, everyone staggering into the theatre lot. Night chill razors through my thin shirt. Clammy drizzle hangs in the air, a haze of drops, shimmery in the orange streetlights. The kind of rain that can't decide if it should disperse into fog or just drop already.

Stage right, Lauren is already hosing off her pebbles. A dark smear of defiled water — it *does* look just like blood — oozes its way toward us.

"Dani," I say. "It's late."

She's sobbing. "Real, it's real, it's totally real …"

"You're drunk. Calm down."

"*Real*, Sam!" She pitches something at my chest.

Mackenzie catches it on the bounce. She drops it, just as fast, with a horrified shriek.

"What the hell?"

"It's a molar." Among Phyll's many remarkable qualities is she's unflappable. She swigs whiskey straight from the bottle and mouths, to me, "No Mitch inside."

"Werewolves," giggles the trombone player, pouncing on the tooth.

Mackenzie startles, screaming again. She's spotted Burt, the kid playing our mafia boss. Must've caught him in her peripheral vision and mistaken him for a wolfman.

Burt's leaning on Phyll's old champagne-coloured Impala, smoking a cigarette with shaking, latex-gloved hands. A pair of pliers sits beside him on the hood of the car, with the red-smeared pump bottle of sterilizing gel from the men's.

The stain on his chest is blood. Crimson Morning or the real deal?

I snatch the discarded tooth as the trombone player starts making wolf noises: "A-wooooooo!" His cronies join in, howling in a jokey way to see if they can further wind up the girls.

"Burt," I shout. He pans his head in my direction, but his eyes fail to hook mine. "Burt!"

"What?"

"Is this yours?"

I hold up the tooth and he quails a little, then leans over the corner of the Impala and starts heaving.

"It's not his," Phyll sighs. Beads of mist have dusted her hair, like pearls. "I'm thinking it came from Mitch."

"Huh?"

"He said something about an impacted wisdom tooth. By his mirror, just now, I found an empty bottle of codeine. You said he'd been a zombie lately, remember?"

"If he had a bad tooth, why not get it yanked?"

"Money?"

"He has a dentist phobia," Mackenzie says. Of course she would know this. "I think a dentist molested him. Or—"

"Some people are just afraid of dentists." Phyll adds a layer of headmistress resonance to her voice. It corks Mackenzie's sordid suspicions.

"A-woooo!" Our werewolf chorus yowls in time to Burt's retching. He groans, shudders, and pushes himself upright. Upright*ish*. The too-familiar stench of vodka barf sours my already charming mood.

If I *was* going to get anyone in the company to perform experimental dentistry on me, it might indeed be Burt. He's a good-natured kid. Steady, strong, reasonably graceful. More to the point, he's got about as much common sense as the plot of your average porn flick.

"He said it'd be easy," he says, opening the latex glove and revealing the busted fragments of another tooth. "Said he'd dope up, forget it all afterward."

Forget. The Rohypnol. My stomach burns. That's some dentist phobia.

Phyll cuts to the chase. "Where'd he go, Burt?"

"Go?" Blink. "He's gone?"

The jazz band starts baying at that point, like hounds on a scent. They've found a foamy glob of blood and saliva at the end of the parking lot.

"This way!" They head to the hospital, loping in inebriated good spirits toward the *Building Condemned* and *No Trespassing* signs.

"Everyone, stop," I shout, but it's not me that pulls them up short at the boundary of lacy, much-abused chainlink. It's Saint Nicholas, patron saint of prostitutes and lying to your kids about Christmas. He's chipped beyond recognition into a one-eyed, glowering totem.

Mackenzie steps through the tattered fence, reaching for his stumpy wrists. I imagine her climbing up into his outstretched arms, assuming Susanna Sabine's final, bloody pose.

To forestall, I say, "I'll go in and look for Mitch."

A chorus of "No way!" and "You can't go by yourself!" and "Come on, we're, like, totally safer in a group."

"Everyone sticks together." Phyll projects with fear-me-God thunder, and they nod obediently. I feel a thrill of doomed, pointless desire. She takes a swig of Jack and nods for me to do the honours.

What can I do? If I tell them it's dangerous, they'll insist on sticking close to me. If I say this is, comparatively speaking, the warm fuzzy playschool of drug dens, it'll just encourage them to make a picnic of it.

"Goddammit," I growl, opening the door.

They troop past me, pulling their phones out, casting inadequate pools of silver light every which way.

Maybe they won't see anything. Maybe the smell will put them off.

The lobby's cleaner than it was a month ago. I used the same hose that Lauren just deployed on her puddle. Still, the layered stench of body fluids and old rot seeping from the corridor and stairwells should trigger a retreat.

Burt gags. And the jazz band stops howling, which is something. I let myself hope …

Then: "Blood," says Lauren. How she picks it out amid the other smudges on the lino, I'll never know.

"Ohmigod, Sammy," Mackenzie breathes.

So much for nobody seeing the foyer walls.

"Sammy, ohmigod, ohmigod!"

The backdrops for the set, the pages of my live-action graphic novel, are painted on the fifteen-foot high walls of the Saint Nick foyer.

Directly across from us is the ultra-rich neighbourhood with its nice houses and big cars. Facing it, behind us, is Hooker Alley. When I was painting it, I had a view of the present-day version, an abandoned, weed-strewn path of broken concrete tied like an umbilicus to the theatre lot.

The kids drift, mothlike, over to my interpretation of the stalker shrine. The latter was a storage room in this very hospital. After the murder, police found it wallpapered in red-smeared pictures of Susanna Sabine.

Flamingo Tinge, Vesuvius Flow, Spice Market, and Crimson Glory glint down at them from floor to ceiling.

Phyll whispers, "It was you who left the clippings in the green room that first day."

I shrug. "Give a bunch of baby actors a self-written project, they'll do something heartfelt and preachy about just saying no, child sexual assault, or stopping the cyberbullies. Been there, you know?"

"This didn't spring from cynicism about the moribund creative state of our youth." For a second, she has the nerve to look sorry for me. "You're not old enough to be so world-weary, Sammy."

Because she's Phyll, I want to explain. My baby sister's obsessed with Susanna, I want to say. I hoped she'd hear about this and give me a call.

There hasn't been a word, you see, not since I forced her ass into rehab. She's three years clean. She's married. Baby's even got a kid of her own now. But I'm the Grinch who stole Christmas, as far as she's concerned. Stuck in the mud. Non grata. The judgmental, ill-tempered, no-fun, overbearing sacrifice to her sobriety. I'm blocked on her Facebook page, her phone. Fenced out.

How is that fair?

All I can do is peer through the cracks, visiting the *Solve Susanna* conspiracy site and making pathetic — theatrical, you might say — attempts to capture either Baby's imagination or her forgiveness.

Instead of spilling any of this, I raise my voice. "Now you've seen that I know the place, maybe you'll wait here while I look for Mitch—"

Too late. They feel safe now. If Sammy can hang out here, obviously, they all can. Anyway, they're immortal, remember? They make for the stairs.

"Don't split up," I shout. "Dammit, wait—"

"Stop playing shepherd, Sammy."

With that, Phyll makes her move, blocking my way by putting strong hands on my shoulders. She's just my type: I've always gone for powerful women. Everything in me but my so-called better judgment leans toward her.

As her lips close in on mine, the waft of alcohol precedes them.

Contact: lightning surge of want from my body's depths, heart pounding. Then, as a whiskey-soaked tongue meets the water and lime on mine, a corresponding flood of despair, revulsion, grief.

She catches her breath, and, moving fast, I slide my fingers between us. Her mouth presses on my knuckles, encountering flecks of charcoal paint, even as our foreheads collide.

"I can't. I'm sorry. I can't."

"Quit acting so damned old, Sammy."

"Ain't just that, doll." I fall back on the Bogey voice again. "I don't mess with married dames."

Small frown. "I'm not—"

"Mister Jack Daniels says differently. Schweetheart."

Two inches from mine, the playful bedroom eyes turn to steel. Face rigid, she steps back.

I'd hoped to hold this off. I wanted to bask in flirtatious summer heat without ever bringing matters to a point where I'd have to say no and get myself locked out.

Phyll hitches her shoulders, settling her coat more firmly. She takes the stairs to the second floor like a martyr mounting the gallows.

The denizens of the hospital are a pretty sedate bunch, by which I mean my hippie friend Sacker keeps them literally sedated. His pet users sleep off their various binges in rooms on the second and third floors. It's practically a safe injection site: a church-based needle exchange swings by with a van twice a week. I used to volunteer, back in the day. Handing out spikes to the junkies, keeping an eye peeled for Baby.

Which is how I got to know Sacker, obviously.

Now actors in clusters of two and three are galumphing through his druggie day camp, whispering loudly, giggling. World's stupidest field trip. *Trainspotting* meets *Scooby Doo*.

So solve the problem, Sammy.

I'm Mitch, I think. I got idiot-bleeping-Burt to pull my tooth. That must be some mighty dentist phobia. Then … did I come to Saint Nick's because it's a hospital?

I'd want to sit, wouldn't I? Hold my aching jaw. I'd want a chair.

Second floor waiting room?

I'm barely in time. My actors have coalesced at the waiting room entrance. They still have their phones raised. I hear the electronic impersonation of a camera shutter.

"That's him?" asks the werewolf trombone player. Hopeful, but not sure.

Mackenzie cuts loose with a shriek. "Ohmigod, they're *feeding!*"

Beyond her, I see the gleaming highlighter outline of Mitch's enormous running shoes, lightning jags of rubber tread flopping to a one-two-one-two beat. A trio of tattered shadows, wraiths, moves over him.

To be fair to Mackenzie, they do look like extras from a vampire movie. And one of the shapes *is* bent close to the kid's throat.

Which is probably why Burt fires his prop gun.

Boom. More screaming, from just about everyone this time. My ears ring. Shadows skitter away from Mitch, morphing into frightened junkies who vanish through the side doors, leaving only Sacker.

Sacker, who is nobly doing CPR on our dentist-fearing Gary Cooper.

"Don't shoot," he screams, clearly terrified. "Peace, man, peace, don't shoot!"

Burt fires again. Bam. Bam. Bam. Fake bullets, deafening noise, real panic. The pitter-patter of running addict feet builds like thunder in the stairwells.

"Cut it out!" Phyll plucks the thing out of Burt's hand.

Sacker's still pumping Mitch. "One. Shit. Three. Four."

"It's not a real gun, Sacks." I cross the floor, kneel beside Mitch, and jam my fingers into his neck. There might be a hint of a pulse.

"What the fuh? Sammy?"

"Is it Rohypnol? Can you OD on that?"

"What. Am I? The Mayo—huh—Clinic?" Sacker's a frail guy, and CPR's more work than you'd think.

"Let me take over," I say. "Listen. Everyone's running for it. The building will be clear before the ambulance and cops arrive. Burt's a dumb shit, and he shouldn't have fired the shots, but nobody's hurt and nobody'll get arrested."

Sacker sucks his teeth. "They'll board the place up."

"You'll get back in. You always do. It's okay, Sacks. Take off. I got this."

The actors are still catching up with current events. "Seriously," says Burt. "You know this guy?"

Sacker draws himself up, throwing my puppies a malevolent glower. Everyone but Phyll steps back. I forget how scary he can seem, with his skeletal frame, perennially red eyes, and silver-yellow dreadlocks. Stalking across the room, he takes the side door out.

My flock creeps closer.

"Mitch okay?" Quavery little-kid voice from Mackenzie.

"Okay? Are you kidding? He's—Which of you asstards is sober enough to call 911 without babbling about vampires or werewolves?"

"I'll call," Phyll says.

Praise bleeding Santa Claus for functional alcoholics. "Everyone go wait out by the statue. Stay together."

An eternity later, maybe just five minutes before the ambulance arrives, Mitch opens his eyes. "Is lack time travel," he says, grinning bloodily, glaze-eyed.

"Yeah, buddy, time travel," I say. "You're gonna be okay."

"Whah happen?"

"You don't want to know," I say. I figure that since he was looking to forget about the tooth extraction, I'm basically speaking truth.

The paramedics come, hefting Mitch out past his fellow actors like a wrapped-up set piece in a Tangerine Sunset blanket. Outside, the drizzle has cleared, and it's almost dawn. Phyll, I see, is conversing with the cops who accompanied the ambulance. Nobody's taking an attitude: her charisma works its usual magic.

I count heads. Danielle is in Saint Nick's shadow, contemplating the pitted marble, the busted arms that once cradled a murdered girl in a fur coat. Her makeup is streaked with tears, and she doesn't look like Lauren Bacall anymore. More like a kid wearing Grandma's best for the school dance.

Burt is all but passed out, latex gloves and all, on the hospital steps.

The jazz kids are smoking cigarettes and texting their friends, and little Mackenzie is chatting up a uniformed patrolman who doesn't look old enough to drive. He's telling her about some car accident, feeding her all the gory details.

"Everyone can go. We have your contact info," announces a patrolman. He casts a significant glance at the *No Trespassing* sign on the hospital's moth-eaten chain link.

With a collective sigh, the group gets moving.

Phyll falls into step beside me. Her hand reaches, out of habit, for the bottle in her pocket. She doesn't take it out.

"You won't reconsider?" she says. "You and me, I mean."

I chew my lip.

"What if I divorced Mr Daniels?"

I can tell it's hard for her to say the words, to even consider conceding. It's flattering, so flattering, to know she wants me enough to consider it.

I should say no. I'm no wide-eyed innocent. I know better. "Bring me a one-year chip, and we'll talk."

"A year?"

"Twelve long, dry months."

"You call that reconsidering?"

Take it or leave it, schweetheart. If I speak, I'll channel Bogey again, and whatever it is — this chance — it'll tear like tissue paper.

I press my lips together, fighting to hold in the flood. We've had enough dramatics tonight without me going to pieces over the things I want and how I wish I didn't want them.

"How do you know if an addict is lying?" Phyll mutters.

So she has tried to quit, at least once. "Their lips are moving. Yeah. I'll be checking with your sponsor."

She lets out a long breath and pulls her trench coat shut, buttoning it with deliberate movements of her strong, elegant fingers. Resigned? Insulted?

She takes out the bottle and hands it to me. I feel that flash of heat between us again, like a holy, cleansing fire. Or, more likely, the kind of fire that just burns.

As we walk away from the hospital, I feel the eyes of the scabrous Saint Nicholas statue, the hook of a judgmental gaze between my shoulder blades. He knows if you've been bad or good, remember.

Then morning sun unfurls over the theatre building, breaking Nick's hold on me as it bathes the young cast of *Cutting Room* in a natural spotlight. Silhouetted against the dawn, they make their bandy-legged way out of the alley, shadows bopping off into a fabulous, newly minted tomorrow.

Mackenzie turns. "You guys coming?"

"Right behind you," I call, enjoying that sense of walking beside Phyll. Of *hoping*, even if I shouldn't, and the pristine breath of the morning on my face.

FEATURE INTERVIEW

AM Dellamonica

Pulp Literature: In 'Wrap Party', you take us behind the scenes of a theatre company, and your blog touches on your background in community theatre. Could you tell us a bit about that and how your experiences did (or did not) play a role in the story?

AM Dellamonica: I spent my literal childhood doing various kinds of amateur performance, including working with backstage crew on plays from *Rashamon* to *Godspell* to *You're a Good Man, Charlie Brown.* My parents were heavily involved in community theatre in the northern Alberta town where I went to grade school, so it started there.

After I left home, I spent a couple seasons doing professional theatre, mostly as a stage manager or lighting technician, but occasionally on stage as either an actor or a singer.

I have built sets, run props, hung lights, written and performed songs, made stage booze, cleaned up stage blood, loaded fake guns, gotten my hair mistakenly sprayed with Lysol (instead of hairspray) once when I was doing *The Children's Hour,* and had my fake child murdered in a medieval pageant recreation … along with all the other extras in *Herod's Massacre of the Innocents.*

The takeaway shouldn't be that I'm unusual or amazing, though. It's that theatre is a colourful and varied subculture to live in!

It can be a big drinking subculture, though, and in the great genetic lottery, I failed to get a heavy drinker gene. So often I have been the most sober person at the cast party, which is part of what 'Wrap Party' is about. At seventeen, as the youngest member in the theatre company, it made me feel unusually conspicuous.

PL: Noir in general asks us to acknowledge human dysfunction and darkness, and 'Wrap Party' shines a light into this bleakness. Your characters claw at decency and wrestle with their passions. What did you enjoy most about creating this world for them?

AMD: I know the noir aesthetic is bleakness with an overlay of fatalism, and I tried to capture that in 'Wrap Party', but I would never want to write something that was completely nihilistic. It feels like hating people, and I don't much care for art or artists that give off a misanthropic vibe.

PL: In Issue 23, your wife, Kelly Robson, described you as "an amazing story doctor." As a story doctor, writing teacher, and recent MFA grad (congrats!), how do you know when a piece of writing is going to pull through, and how do you know when it's a 'do not resuscitate'?

AMD: For my own work, I know the story has reached a do not resuscitate point when I lose interest in it. It's a particular kind of feeling, like having all the water go out of a hose. It just withers on the vine. It hurts, but I don't feel much doubt that it's gone.

What is sometimes interesting as an instructor is working on a story with a student whose piece isn't quite there yet but who isn't ready to let go. You have to wait until they are ready to move onto the next work while trying to find ways to make the critiquing process useful and ensuring they don't feel they got their dreams crushed.

PL: What is your favourite part of working with new writers? And what do you find the most challenging?

AMD: Seeing new writers get better is such a thrill! You never know who's going to come back from a critique session galvanized, with a piece that has taken a huge leap forward. When you get to work with someone for a stretch of time, coming back to their work can require more and more rigour— it gets harder to find things to advise them about because they are doing so incredibly well!

I don't have human children, but it must be a little like seeing your offspring win Olympic medals.

The most interesting challenge can be that within any given group of aspiring writers, there's going to be a huge range of experience and ability. You'll have someone who is just about ready to sell their work and someone who has really just started and who might not even be in a space to hear if it's imperfect. You get people in the middle, who are doing brilliantly on description and yet have abysmal dialogue… And yet you sort of have to teach to the room, trying to find something that everyone can use to come away better at their craft.

PL: *On your blog, you mention your visit to the Museum of English Rural Life and your discovery of the BBC Historical Farm Series. Are these forays into farm life research for an upcoming project?*

AMD: Yes! My current novel, *Gamechanger* (which is out under the name LX Beckett) is set in 2101, in a future where we've managed to roll back some of the damage we've done to the climate and are continuing to work on remediation.

I'm now working on the sequel, *Dealbreaker,* and there's an immense amount about both rationing and heavily regulated farming (in the World-War-II, UK sense of the word). *Dealbreaker* has an etymologist who is trying to bioengineer a better locust as a protein crop (locusts are high in cholesterol, and lack one essential amino acid). That character's parent is a career farmer who has been out working a hydroponics facility near Saturn.

PL: *As an award-winning author yourself, which authors do you turn to for inspiration and insight?*

AMD: My wife, Kelly Robson, is one of the most innovative and inspiring people I know! And some of the other writers I have been reading lately are Amal El-Mohtar, Max Gladstone, Tamsyn Muir, Annalee Newitz, Kellan Szpara, Rebecca Kuang, and Rebecca Roanhorse. We are in something of a platinum age of intersectional and aspirational SF, and I am eating it all up with a big spoon and a delighted grin on my face.

THE EXTRA: FRANKIE RAY ROLLS INTO TINSELTOWN

Mel Anastasiou

Mel Anastasiou *writes mysteries, including the Fairmount Manor Mysteries and the Hertfordshire Pub Mysteries, available at pulpliterature.com. For her novel* Stella Ryman and the Fairmount Manor Mysteries, *Mel won a Literary Titan Gold Book Award and was longlisted for the Leacock Memorial Medal for Humour. In Part 3 of the Monument Studios Mystery* The Extra, *Frankie Ray and Connie Mooney reach Hollywood in their stolen rattletrap, with unexpected extra cargo — a mendacious movie mogul and his gun-shot son. A power struggle at the highest levels and a gun under the seat propel the can-do heroines to a rocky start in Tinseltown, 1934.*

OLLYW

THE EXTRA:
A MONUMENT STUDIOS MYSTERY

CHAPTER ONE

This was not how Frankie had planned to arrive in Los Angeles.

Not with King Samson, head of Monument Studios, hunched over the wheel of the Model A. Not with Frankie in the rumble seat, hanging on with both hands and jouncing madly with every turn as midday wore on to afternoon.

Frankie said, "I wish we didn't have to drive so fast."

"You go ahead and wish," King Samson said. "I'm in a hurry. I've got to put myself between Marietta and my director before she drives him crazy with her woman-director opinions. *Or* he up and quits."

"I'm cold and windblown," Connie said, "and bounced halfway to old age."

"Tin-can it," Samson said. "The two of you have groused and fidgeted ever since we pulled over for coffee and doughnuts three hours ago. Cold coffee."

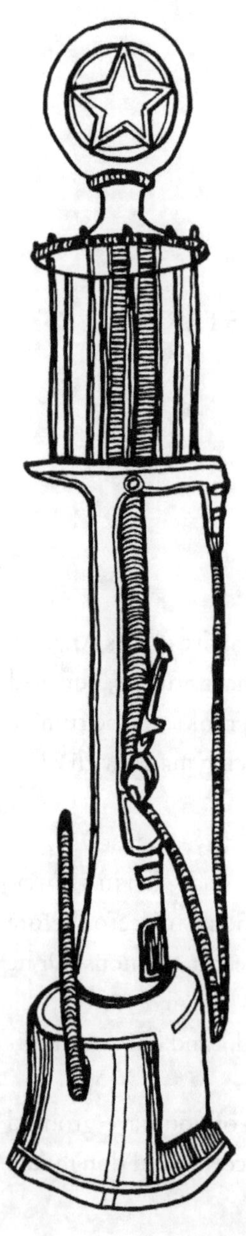

"Tasty doughnuts," Frankie murmured. "And my cocoa was plenty hot."

The head of Monument Studios changed gears with a roar.

With Samson doing the lion's share of the driving, they stopped only when the tanks showed empty. Once the tanks were filled, they'd torn past Burma-Shave ads so quickly that they missed half the punch lines. Now it was Thursday afternoon, and as California deepened around them, Samson refused to give up the wheel, ripping through grim forests of oil wells and storming seas of pastel bungalows edged with white picket fences.

Frankie wiggled her knees around on the rumble seat and thought about things. She thought, for example, that even though he'd paid for their food and fuel all the way south, King Samson's shoe was too heavy on the gas. Connie never learned to speed up when she was taking a corner, like Frankie did. And Leo, with his wounded shoulder, never took the wheel at all. But they'd made it almost all the way to Hollywood, and that fact alone made her smile until the wind slapped a small bit of something into her eye.

She squeezed her eyes half-shut and blinked until they were clear. Palm trees along the side of the road cast shadows that flicked over her like scenes from a stuttering movie projector. Every so often an oil derrick, smack in the middle of the road, lowed and creaked as they passed, and for a moment or two the whole world smelled like petroleum. Frankie almost lost her hat to the wind, staring goggle-eyed at ticky-tack businesses like the Coffeepot Diner—shaped, by heaven, like a coffeepot. On the left side of the road stood midnight auto supply garages, shiny with stacked hubcaps. On the right lay junkyards, prickly with scrap iron. Where, Frankie asked herself, was the grandeur? Where was the glamour?

Where was Hollywood?

She pictured her father, glowering over the rim of his sherry glass. *"Fool of a girl, look to the hills, whence cometh my help."*

Even from his bed a thousand miles to the north, her father was right. Frankie looked to the hills, and there it was. She nudged Connie. Heads swivelling, they gaped at the huge crooked letters standing chalk-white against the green and brown hills above the city.

The huge sign read *Hollywoodland*. Frankie was so overcome by the sight that she had to remind herself to breathe.

Samson leaned forward and jutted out his chin, both hands on the wheel of the Model A. They sped like an arrow straight down the street to the end of the road. Ahead, the road widened into a palm-lined avenue, busy with traffic.

A smaller sign on the roadside read *Sunset Boulevard.*

The end of the road. Frankie could hardly believe they'd arrived. She could more easily believe that the four of them would sit in this car, in a tangle of mutual help and enmity, to the end of time. But they'd made it, and straight ahead of them stood a pair of gates as tall and golden as the gates of song and story. Shining letters across a great wall read *Monument Studios,* and beside the gates there loomed a pair of radiant statues.

"Are they supposed to be movie stars?" Connie wondered aloud.

"They must be," Frankie answered. But when she looked again, she saw the angels' wings arching out of the shoulders.

King Samson drove straight at the Monument Studio angels. Frankie hardly had time to brace herself with both hands before he threw on the brakes at the studio gates.

"Thank all the gods I'm back," Samson growled. "Hope to heaven I've still got a director."

Connie stood up and leaned over the back seat. She gestured at the golden angels and the sign that read *Monument Studios*. "Is all this really yours, Mr Samson?"

"Earned twice over." King Samson yanked the key out of the ignition and struggled to untangle his jacket from the gearshift. Something thudded to the floor of the car, but he didn't seem to notice. "All I want is control of my own movie in my own goddamn studio. Is that too much to ask?"

"You're the boss, so I guess not," Connie said. "Say, can we come in?"

King Samson turned to face Connie. He repeated, "Can you come in? You mean, into the *studios*?"

"*May* we come in?" Frankie asked. "Please. We'd love to see around a real studio and everything."

King Samson slumped back down into his seat. His posture was that of a man who had been handed one burden too many by an improvident and unfeeling fate.

He said, "You two groused at me for almost a thousand miles. You argued and shoved like *I* was nobody and *you* were nobody—as if we were all nobodies together. And I put up with it. I tolerated you young upstarts on the long road south. And now we're in Hollywood. And I'm a producer and studio owner. What are you?"

Frankie said, "We're somebodies who did you a favour, Mr Samson. That's who we are."

"They're within their rights there, Dad." Leo followed Connie out of the car, holding his gun-shot shoulder. "We owe these girls a thank-you."

"Thank you." Samson smacked the steering wheel with both palms, and the Model A trembled. "Thank you, impertinent and complaining girls from the undiscovered armpit of nowhere. And now I suppose you want me to make you both big movie stars as a return favour? Would that be an appropriate gesture in return for a lousy little lift in your old rattletrap?"

He banged his fist on the door. Frankie reached across his broad middle section and unlatched the door handle. She said, "Actually, it's my father's car."

Connie added, "And we don't want anything from you, you old grouch."

"Shush, Connie. Don't burn our bridges." Frankie addressed the producer's back as he climbed out of the car. "Mr Samson, we don't want anything from you except that you honour your verbal contract with Connie to give her a little part in your movie. Not because we gave you a ride, but because you know from your experience finding talent that she *has* something."

King Samson replied, "Somebody once said that a verbal contract isn't worth the paper it's written on, girls." He must have seen their stricken faces, because he added, "Look. If you're good enough, you'll make it."

"You ought to owe us a favour, Mr Samson," Connie said.

"Sure I *ought*," Samson said to Frankie, "if life was fair. But it so happens you have to work for what you get, girls. So go to work. Learn how to act. Catch my eye, or better still, my director's eye. Get singled out for your chance. I won't hold the last two days against you. Even better—I'll forget we ever met."

He turned away from them, looked up, and froze.

Frankie shaded her eyes against the afternoon sun and followed his gaze, past the guard's glassed-in kiosk, past the high walls, to a window in what must have been the office block for Monument Studios. Framed in the window, star actress Marietta

Valdes looked down at them. She gestured to somebody Frankie couldn't see and stepped out of view. Star actor Gilbert Howard took her place. He touched the tip of his finger to the side of his beautifully arched Roman nose as the window blind dropped and hid him from sight.

"Look at those two. Marietta and Gilbert, fresh as fish and cocky as hell after a meeting with my director. They're trying to steal my movie. Goddamnglamorous pirates, that's what they are." King Samson banged a fist on the hood of the Model A and stumped off in the direction of the studio gates. He flung the guard in the glass kiosk a jerk of his big dark head. A small door cut into the larger gates opened to admit him and shut behind him.

Frankie turned to Leo. "Is there any chance he'll repent of his temper and hire Connie?"

Leo screwed up his face in an apparent attempt to cheer them up. "Who knows? You're in Hollywood, after all. Anything is possible."

"Applesauce." Connie turned her back. "You're all full of applesauce."

Frankie was inclined to agree. The temperamental King Samson was one thing. But, as the girls had given a much-needed lift to a good fellow like Leo, she'd rather expected that he would, at least, offer to talk to his father on their behalf. However, she had to bear in mind that Leo was the picture of a son under his father's thumb.

Frankie reached out to pat Leo on the shoulder but remembered his gunshot wound just in time. "Don't mind Connie. She's just disappointed. I never really believed that she could have a studio contract handed to her in the middle of the drive south, before she even stepped foot in Hollywood. Still, we're bound to have some good luck soon …"

She trailed off, for Leo's attention had wandered from the conversation to something on the far side of Sunset Boulevard. Frankie checked over her shoulder, but the street was empty except for the parked cars along the sidewalk. "Leo?"

Leo started. "Sorry, what did you say?"

"You must be looking forward to seeing your fiancée."

"Sure I am."

What was the fellow staring at? There was nothing across the road but a large Spanish-style mansion, its tile roof shining a bright orange-gold in the late afternoon sun. With its streaming bougainvillea and rattling palm trees, the lot covered most of the block across the road.

Connie said, "Hey ya, Frankie, what do you say we live in a house like that?" She pointed at the mansion.

Leo looked from the mansion to Connie. "Pardon? That house over there?"

"Oh, Leo, are you with us after all?" Connie sang, waving at him with a mock cheeriness that would have sent Leo's father—or Frankie's—into a purple rage.

"Listen, I've got to go. Good luck in the movies, you two." Leo walked away toward the studio doors that had recently opened for King Samson. Did Leo's fiancée work at Monument Studios? Perhaps she was an actress. Frankie hadn't thought to ask.

Behind Leo's back, Connie stuck out her tongue at him. "Bye bye, Leo. Don't take any wooden nickels."

Frankie said, "Darn it all, Connie. You are sticking your tongue out at the only nice person we've met on the road to

Hollywood. Who knows when we'll find another one? You might try not burning every bridge we cross."

"Where's your sense of humour gone?" Connie demanded. "Did you leave it in an Oregon café as a tip for the waitress?"

"Oh, tin-can it," Frankie said, in an approximation of King Samson's cantankerous tones. The two girls leaned on the cooling Model A. The breeze was worth appreciating, even if it was only one degree cooler than her skin.

The man in the guard box outside Monument Studios leaned out his little window. His hat was so big that it rested on his ears. He cracked his gum with a sound like distant gunfire. "You there, move that car."

Frankie felt in her pockets. "King Samson took our car key."

"Holy Moses," Connie said. "King Samson is quite the old stinker. Hey, Mr Guard, can you go inside the studio and get us our key back?"

The guard said, "If you gals had any brains, you'd have an extra key."

Frankie admitted that they did not have a spare key. "Could you ask Leo Samson to get the key from his father?"

"Please," Connie added. Most often, that was all she needed to say to a man, but Frankie imagined there might be quite a few lovely girls saying *please* to the guard at the gates of Monument Studios.

"It's beyond my listed duties," the guard said. "Look, you kids better move that car fast."

Frankie asked, "Would you please give us a push onto the street at least?"

"I don't even leave this booth at gunpoint." The guard chewed away at his gum.

The girls peered into the golden west to see a uniformed police officer, ticket pad in hand, working the shining line of cars along Sunset Boulevard.

Connie said, "What if we had a flat tire? The cop couldn't make us move the car then. Go on, Frankie, stab the tire with your hatpin again."

Frankie sucked her top lip. "We have no further spare tires, Connie."

"Oh, yeah." Connie slumped against the car door. "Am I stupid?"

"No," Frankie said. "You're just a complicated thinker."

The guard wiped his nose on his sleeve. "Sure. And anyway, you got the looks. But cops are as cold as ice. Lemme show you something."

Either the guard now revealed his gentlemanly side, or else his regard for Connie's good looks outweighed his duty to his glass kiosk, for he left his post and walked over to the Model A. "You girls might as well bark at the moon as beg King Samson for your key back. But that don't matter. Watch and learn." Reaching under the dashboard, he pulled two wires, seemingly at random, from behind the ignition keyhole. "Wind the fair ends together. Press the starter button. Got it?"

The Model A started up beautifully.

"I think so, thanks," Frankie said. She did have it. Or she was almost sure she did.

"If you separate the wires again," he added, "she'll stop."

Frankie studied the wires. She saw how to separate them, all right, although you'd think touching them would give you a nasty old shock.

As the guard returned to his kiosk, Frankie's fatigue fell away. She felt that she could do anything and handle any circumstance.

Already she was not the same girl who had left Vancouver on Saturday night. For a start, she was a far better driver. And now she had even gained the skills required to jump-start a car.

Connie snapped a salute to the guard. She hopped up behind the wheel. Frankie reluctantly took the passenger seat.

"Let's find some place to sleep tonight," Frankie said. "It had better be cheap, though."

"Are you bananas?" Connie put the Model A in gear. "We just got here. Let's drive all over Hollywood."

Frankie helped Connie fiddle with the choke. "I tell you what," she said. "We can do both. Let's drive around Hollywood and keep our eyes open for a place to stay."

Connie grinned and leaned into one of her famous swinging U-turns, close as breathing to the fenders of a few inconveniently speedy sedans. As they turned, something small and heavy slid from one side to the other underneath the seat of the car.

Ahead of them, the street was thick with cars, but on the sidewalk opposite Monument Studios there was only one pedestrian. This was a California blonde in tennis whites. The girl was so pretty she looked as if, instead of growing up here, she had simply ripened like a peach in the perfect California weather. Connie sped up.

The girl stepped out onto the road in front of the car.

Frankie was too startled to shout a warning and too late to grab the wheel. Connie slammed on the brakes, but there was no time to dodge the girl in tennis whites. The front bumper caught her hip and sent her sprawling onto the curb. Connie jammed the car out of gear while Frankie pulled up on the brake with both hands. Frankie scrambled out onto the road and almost got herself knocked down in the blast of wind generated by a panel truck. The blonde sat down on the curb next to the back wheel of the Model A.

Frankie knelt at her side. "Sit still. We'll take you to the hospital."

"Don't." The girl pulled her tennis skirt straight across her thighs and buried her face in her hands. "I'm fine."

Connie said, "Were you in dreamland or something? You might have been killed."

Frankie sent Connie a look. In their secret code she hissed, "*Anna Karenina. Juliet. Ophelia.*"

Connie took a moment with the code. "Gosh. Like Cleopatra? Only a car instead of a poisonous snake?"

The girl ground the heels of her hands against her eyes. "I'm just lucky, I guess. I mean, I'm lucky that you two are such good drivers."

Frankie shook her head. Something had to be said, or this pretty young woman would go and throw herself beneath the wheel of another car. She took the girl's hands gently in her own and pulled them away from her face. "Getting yourself hit by a car is a terrible way to go, don't you think? I mean for those you leave behind. And so hard on the one who mows you down in her vehicle."

The girl looked Frankie in the eye. "I wouldn't kill myself. I was singing to myself. 'Dora Heart'. You know how the chorus goes. *Hi de hi de hi . . .*"

Frankie didn't believe her for a moment. Still, saying so was no way to cheer up a suicide. "Around the world," Frankie said lightly, "or down the block, the song's the same."

"'Dora Heart'? Hazel's kids love that song," Connie said.

Frankie put her arm around the girl's shoulder. Poor kid. What would drive a lovely California girl to take her own life?

Beautiful women had so many opportunities. Even plain women had options. Even women somewhere in between, like Frankie, had possibilities. "What's your name?"

"Puddin' tain." The girl winced. "Sorry. It's Billie Starr."

"Pretty name." Marietta Valdes's words echoed: *Nothing is as it seems in Hollywood.* Frankie supposed there was nothing wrong with picking out your own name, especially if you'd been slapped at birth with something like Etta or Lally. Even her own name, Francesca, wasn't everybody's cup of tea. She wondered, though, why *Billie?* Perhaps after Billie Dove. She fully understood why the girl would choose a moniker like *Starr.*

Billie Starr said, "I've got everything to look forward to, you know." Her eyes strayed to the golden angels guarding the gates to Monument Studios. "I had a contract for a little while."

Connie said, "Sure. You're beautiful."

The girl shook her head. "Everybody's beautiful. I've got talent, though."

"You've got that *something,*" Connie assured her. "Right, Frankie?"

"Sure. Star quality, like Connie here. Look, Billie," Frankie said, "when you've got so much going for you already, all you have to do is work hard. King Samson himself said so." It was one interpretation of the producer's words, anyway. "You'll make it someday."

"I want to make it now. While I'm at my best." Billie Starr's eyes lit up, and Frankie saw how truly lovely this girl was.

"Me, too," Connie said glumly.

They helped Billie to her feet. Frankie smelled the drink on the girl now.

"Thanks. I do feel better, girls." Billie Starr stood in the shadow of a palm. She brushed at the grey streaks on her skirt. Behind her, bougainvillea blazed pink against the white walls of the Spanish-style mansion. "Come on in, and I'll make you a little drink."

"Okay," Connie said.

"Just a soda, though," Frankie said.

But at a shout from across the road, the three young women turned.

On the curb on the opposite side of Sunset Boulevard, Leo gestured wildly with his good arm. "Stay out of that house."

Billie Starr shot him a nasty look and walked stiffly toward the big wooden doors of the mansion. Connie followed after. Frankie hesitated, looking back at Leo. He'd never before appeared so animated, not even when Gilbert Howard had shot him in the shoulder.

Leo said, "Come back, please, girls. Listen, I've got the key to your car."

The heavy doors thudded shut, leaving Connie standing just outside. Connie slapped the door with the flat of her hand. "Billie just shut the door in my face."

"She's not herself, that's all. Listen, we need that car key." Frankie waved at Leo, who was moving in their direction on the other side of the street. "Although I think we should leave the car running, just in case."

"But you could jump-start it again, like the guard showed us."

Frankie reviewed the guard's instructions. *First find some of the wires, then press the starter button. Or the clutch. Not the brake, that's for certain.* "Yes. Well, let's leave it running, to save time." She eyed the traffic, fierce and smoky like Tolstoy's trains. "And let's not have any *Anna Karenina* stuff, either."

Traffic was so wild that Frankie thought they'd have to stand at that curb until night fell before they'd get a break in the flow of cars. It was as if every vehicle ever assembled in America, every rattling trailer and chugging truck, had been lined up around the corner just waiting for two Canadian girls to try to cross to the other side. She waved a hand to Leo to show him that they intended to cross, but in the meantime there was nothing for it but to stand and watch until traffic slowed as one after another half-dozen battered vehicles turned the corner by Monument Studios.

These rattletraps rolled by piled with luggage. Old men sat at the wheel, women at their sides, young men and children perched on running boards and bumpers, hanging on by the ropes that secured their luggage. There was a rocking chair strapped to a couple of old mattresses on top of the first car. Was that a hip bath tied up on a car roof?

"Okies," Frankie told Connie. *Poor as gruel*, her father said of them. "Looking for work, I guess. I wonder if they'll get jobs in the orange groves."

"The Okies should try to get work in the movies, like us," Connie said.

One of the drivers, shirtsleeves rolled up, let loose a wolf whistle.

Connie whistled back. "We're really in California, aren't we?"

"Bet your bottom dollar." *This is Sunset Boulevard. That up there is a clear blue Hollywood sky. The air is velvet, and the flowers blaze in the sunlight. But a beautiful girl just tried to kill herself, and chances are that the Okie kid with the friendly grin and the whistle won't eat his fill tonight.*

In a week or two, a month or two, would this new world do that to Connie and her? There were a million hard-luck stories everywhere, even in Hollywood. But she didn't believe anything bad could happen to her or to Connie — didn't believe it deep inside, where a person keeps her luck.

As if to prove Frankie right, heaven sent down a break in the traffic. She seized Connie by the hand. The two of them dashed for dear life from one side of the road to the other.

Chapter Two

"You girls have got to be more careful crossing Sunset Boulevard. You could get yourselves killed." Leo Samson stood at the curb, still in his yellow suit with its bloody shoulder and grimy cuffs. Above him towered the angel gates and office buildings of Monument Studios. The sky was deepening with the afternoon, but the air was still warm.

Leo held out the car key to Frankie. "I took it back from Dad."

"Oh, Leo, we don't need a key," Connie said. "Any mutt knows how to jump-start a car."

"And then do you know how to put the wires back together so that you can use this key?"

"The guard showed us how to do everything." Frankie took the car key from him. And, even dog-tired in a strange city and without a place to lay her head, it was easy to recognize this as one of those moments in life where she should count her blessings. Frankie thanked him for the car key and slipped it into her pocket.

Checking his watch, Leo nodded. Although he was nothing like Champ in appearance, Frankie recognized the look in Leo's eye. He was the picture of a polite man with somewhere else he wants to be.

"Look here," he said. "Where are you girls staying for the night? You got somewhere safe to go?"

Frankie wondered whether they shouldn't park the Model A by the side of the road and sleep in it for free. She thought of the Okies, without homes or money, and made a fist around the little wad of dollars in her pocket. She began, "We'll buy a newspaper and check the advertisements—"

Connie interrupted. "Oh, we'll just drive around looking for signs. *Room to Rent.* You can find one anywhere."

"All around the world," Frankie added.

"Or down the block." Connie jerked her thumb at the far side of the road where the mansion stood, framed by palm trees. "Maybe us two Vancouver girls will spend our first night in a fancy place like that. Maybe we'll ask Billie Starr whether we could stay overnight with her."

Leo started and shook his head vehemently, but Frankie thought that sleeping overnight with Billie Starr was a brilliant solution. "We'll trot across and ask her."

Leo said, "You shouldn't. It's . . ."

"It's what?" Frankie asked. "I really think everyone should finish their sentences."

"Or go to prison," Connie agreed. "It's very annoying in a man."

"That's not a Hollywood mansion." Leo looked about ready to melt into the sidewalk. "That's a brothel."

Traffic tore past, lifting the hem of Leo's jacket and stirring the girls' skirts while the three of them stared at the house. Frankie had seen a brothel before—the time she fetched home her neighbour Irene's husband from a raddled old building in Vancouver's dock area.

"An actual brothel?" she ventured. "Right across the street from Monument Studios? You mean to tell us Billie Starr is not an actress after all … she's a …" *Prostitute* seemed a harsh word for such a pretty girl as Billie.

"… a streetwalker?" Connie finished for Frankie. "And that's a house full of them? I can't believe it."

Leo nodded, and in his eyes Frankie saw all the sorrow a young man in a yellow suit could contain.

She said, "Gosh. It's the danger of Hollywood, isn't it?"

"It's one of 'em." Leo dug into his pocket and once again held out his hand. Another key lay in the flat of his palm. "Take this, Frankie. It's for a bungalow at Paradise Gardens, Villa 7B, just a little further down Sunset Boulevard."

Frankie stared at the key as he held it out to her.

"We mustn't," she said.

"Mustn't we?" Connie asked.

Frankie said, "We both know that we mustn't. Thanks anyway."

Connie sniffed and accepted the house key from Leo. Frankie retrieved it and returned it to Leo.

Leo frowned. "Listen, Frankie, you gave me and Dad a lift when we needed one." He touched his injured arm. "You helped me out when Gilbert Howard shot me."

"Be that as it may—" Frankie began.

Leo flung his arms wide open then hunched up his wounded shoulder. "Damn it all, I'm not offering to pay the rent. All you women jump to the wrong conclusions."

Connie glared at Frankie. "*I* don't. Kindness is human nature."

Frankie scowled back. While keeping within the borders of his fatherly duties, Sheridan D had done what he could to substitute for her absent mother. Meanwhile, Connie's mother had taught Frankie the facts of life and general mores at the same time as she'd taught Connie, with varying results. And both parents had made one thing very clear: a young woman did not accept a gift from a man who was not family or fiancé. There was no way around the rule. Not so much as a box of candied peel was allowed. Certainly not a bed for the night. Because although Connie's mother and Frankie's dad never specified what a woman would owe—it would, one reasoned, depend on the sort of man in the case—she would owe the man something.

Frankie said, "Human nature is exactly why we can't accept that key."

A smartly dressed woman banged through the door from Monument Studios and pointed her finger at the guard in his glass kiosk. "I can break all those bastards, Dickie."

"Yes, Miss Carver." The guard leaned out of the kiosk window and touched two fingers to the brim of his cap. "Not me, though."

The woman patted the guard's cheek. "No, Dickie, you'll be happy forever here in your little glass coffin outside the studio gates."

Miss Carver. Frankie stopped worrying about a place to sleep. *Blanche Carver.* Blanche Carver was the star columnist for the *Los Angeles Morning Gazette.* The other two famous gossip columnists, Hedda Hopper and Louella Parsons, might have slightly larger readerships, but they couldn't compete with Blanche Carver's looks or her excellent grammar. Frankie shuffled her feet in wonder at seeing, in person, this former Ziegfeld chorus girl who wrote the Hollywood gossip column *Tell the Truth.* Connie stood, open-mouthed, and Frankie swallowed hard to steady herself. Back home, the only people she ever recognized on the street were fellow teachers, neighbourhood children, and members of her father's former congregation. But it seemed that in Hollywood, there were giants everywhere.

The guard said, "I heard that under your suit jacket there's a heart of gold, Miss Carver."

"A heart of gold?" Blanche Carver shook a finger at him. "Not me. All I want is to write a good story for the *Gazette,* and for that you don't need a heart—or interviews. Everybody lies, including King ruddy Samson."

Still scowling, the columnist turned to face Frankie, Connie, and Leo. She said to Leo, "My darling child. You look terrible. Who's been bleeding on your jacket?"

"Nobody, Mom." Leo put his cheek against hers and she gave it a hard peck of a kiss.

Frankie could have kicked herself for forgetting this bit of Hollywood dynastic history. Anybody who read *Movie Mirror* or *Screenplay* knew that Blanche Carver had been King Samson's first wife. Leo's mother would be a valuable ally to have in Hollywood, almost as important as King Samson. If only Connie could make an impression on the columnist. Frankie wondered how best to begin. But before she could set her mind to answer this delicate question, the columnist stepped back from her son and looked from Connie to Frankie.

"What are these, Leo? More aspiring actresses for the movie mill?" Blanche walked around Connie as if she were a statue in a park. "Well, this one's got something."

Leo nodded. "Reminds you of Janet Gaynor, doesn't she?"

"I don't look even an inch like Janet Gaynor," Connie protested.

"She's a 'Gaynor' all right, Leo. Like the last three or four you brought in." Blanche Carver patted Connie's bright hair. "Actress types come in weather patterns, like hurricanes. We get a storm of redheads and then a calm of blondes."

Boldly, Frankie spoke up. "Where does that leave us brunettes, Miss Carver?"

"Lowering our necklines." Blanche Carver's golden hair gleamed as bright as the angels on the gates overhead.

Frankie shook her head. Another unhelpful giant in the business. Considering how much these people knew about getting ahead in Hollywood, they certainly offered little assistance to a newcomer.

Leo said, "Look, Mother, will you vouch for me with these girls? They seem to think I'm on the make. I'm trying to get them a place at Paradise Gardens."

"Good for you, girls. Mind you, Paradise Gardens is one hell of a nice place, and my son Leo's an honourable fellow. But I'm sure you're right to refuse him."

"It's just that he's a man, and we can't accept——" Frankie began.

"These are the rules of life, I know," Blanche Carver interrupted. "I don't live by them, myself. I live by the truth in a town full of lies. And a lot of liars made up the rules of life, as far as I can see."

Connie took a step forward. "Miss Carver, I want some advice about making it here in Hollywood. And please don't tell us to get on the road and go home."

The columnist said, "Advice? Here's some advice for you: all that young girls like you have to offer to Hollywood is a saleable pulchritude. Therefore, keep it on display and locked up tight."

Frankie and Connie exchanged looks. Their parents had taught them much the same.

"And listen," Blanche Carver added. "Forget your damned small-town rules. If you can't change your habits and attitudes for Hollywood, lord knows Hollywood won't change for you. That's my advice, free of charge. You won't get anything else for free in this town."

"Those two pieces of advice don't match up," Connie pointed out.

Frankie said, "Be quiet, Connie. At least she didn't tell us to hie ourselves home to Vancouver. Thanks, Miss Carver."

But the columnist was no longer listening. She had turned to her son. "Darling Leo, take me out to dinner soon someplace swank. After you see my doctor about your shoulder. And throw that yellow suit in the trash."

Without a farewell, she walked five steps away along the sidewalk and then stopped. With all the statuesque dignity of the Ziegfeld chorus dancer she had once been, she turned again and inclined her golden head to Frankie and Connie.

"You kids will fit in well at Paradise Gardens. You remind me of myself, when I'd just arrived in Hollywood. I remember stumbling into this town, my two friends and me, with a battered case bumping the backs of my legs, looking for a place to lay my curly head. And I remember how life took its own turns no matter how hard I hauled on the wheel." Hands in her pockets, Blanche Carver rocked on her heels. "Roads run both ways. Right, Leo?"

She didn't wait for an answer. Raising a hand to the guard as he leaned out of his kiosk, the columnist snapped her way along the sidewalk, smart and boyish in her trouser suit. She slid into the driver's side of a tan and red roadster with whitewalls.

The roadster pulled out into the Sunset Boulevard traffic. Once it was gone, Frankie experienced a burst of unreality, as if the whole trip south was one of her youthful imaginings and she was really back home, sitting on her back porch, and dreaming about Hollywood. Soon she would return to real life. She would water her red geranium and warm up her father's radio in expectation of a happy evening with Jack Benny and his studio orchestra. She would sit on the porch and lean against her fiancé Champ while he smoked Camel cigarettes.

But as soon as she took a deep breath, the memory of her life in Vancouver gave way again to the reality of California. The air here was nothing like the air back home. It was warm and dry with no scent of wet soil. Here on the famous Sunset Boulevard, palm trees waved in jagged symmetry. She said, "Okay, let's find a place to sleep tonight."

"No." Connie took the key to the place in Paradise Gardens back from Leo and pocketed it. "It's time to join the modern world and face the facts of life, Frankie. Miss Carver is right. This is 1934. We're in Hollywood, and I'm done with the old rules."

Frankie countered, "If we were in a Hollywood movie script, and if we took an inappropriate gift, round about two-thirds of the way through the show, payment would be exacted from us in some unexpectedly dire way."

Connie said, "But in the movies, your father would not keep sherry under the bed and your mother would never have walked away when you were a baby."

In the second's pause that followed this statement, Connie appeared to regret her outburst. But Connie never apologized. She only added, "Anyway, you're a respectable girl. An engaged young woman. You're old enough to think for yourself."

The trouble was that everything Connie had said was true.

Frankie turned to Leo. "It's 1934. We accept the key. With thanks."

Connie breathed, "Huzzah."

Frankie slipped the key into her pocket. She looked up and down Sunset Boulevard. It was only one street among many in Hollywood. "Where do we find Paradise Gardens?"

Leo gestured with his good arm. "Follow Sunset Boulevard a few minutes west, that-a-way. Paradise Gardens is one gate past the Garden of Allah. Good luck to you both."

Here at last was another break in the traffic. Frankie and Connie thanked Leo and darted back across the road to where the Model A hummed to itself at the curb. Frankie climbed into the driver's seat, and for once Connie didn't argue. They turned their heads and regarded the brothel where Billie Starr had so recently slammed the door on them.

"Don't stare," Frankie hissed. "Billie might be looking out."

"Who would do that?" Connie asked. "Who would work in a brothel? Not me. At least a girl could sling bacon and eggs somewhere."

Frankie said, "Such a thing will never happen to you and me." She remembered again the time she'd gone looking in downtown Vancouver for her neighbour Irene's husband. Frankie had followed a bit of gossip into a lobby that smelled like rum and Coca-Cola. There she had met a madam with heavy eyebrows and a cash box in her lap. The madam — like Frankie's father — had been listening to Jack Benny on the radio. The "lady of the evening" Irene's husband visited looked about seventeen years old, with her hair combed straight back and tied as if by a mother's hand, a grubby strap showing in the armhole of her blouse. The girl had asked Frankie if she swooned for Bing Crosby. At some point in her life that young girl must have decided, *I'll do that. I'll work in a brothel.*

Frankie leaned over the steering wheel and, with hardly a whisper of complaint from the gears, she pulled away from the curb.

She wouldn't look back at the brothel, but as she drove, she glanced into her rear-view mirror at the angels at the gates of Monument Studios. She had always known Hollywood could make a beautiful girl into a movie star, but not that the same city could turn an equally lovely girl into a streetwalker.

"Billie had a contract." Connie sucked on her upper lip.

"Everybody's story is different."

"I know that back home you thought I was special."

"Everybody did and still does," Frankie assured her. "You're so special that you almost hit it big on the road to Hollywood. But you know what you need to do now, Connie."

"What? Search for another sock-foot movie producer on the side of the road?"

Frankie shook her head. "Do what King Samson told us. Work. For once in your life, you're going to have to go to work like a hopeful girl does when there are hundreds and thousands of other girls trying to get what she wants."

"But if I've got the star quality they're looking for … ?"

Frankie slowed down as a huge black truck tore past them. Her teeth rattled, and she slowed a little more, just to calm down. Behind her, a car horn sounded.

Connie put her foot over Frankie's on the gas, and the Model A sped up.

Connie removed her foot. "I want to succeed, or break my heart trying. Because I'd rather break my heart and try than get married to some fellow or other and live a stupid ordinary old life like … I forget what I was going to say."

Frankie slid her finger into the ring in her pocket and rubbed the diamond chip with her thumb. She slipped it off again.

She looked back along the palm-lined boulevard in time to see Leo in his yellow suit step out into the busy traffic and lope across the road toward the brothel door.

Frankie said nothing to Connie. They had faced enough dark mysteries of life for one day.

The angels guarding the gates of Monument Studios cast their long shadows down Sunset Drive, and Frankie looked over her shoulder again to see whether, in perspective, they appeared protective or even welcoming. She thought they did not; the gilded eyes were too scornful and heavy-lidded, and the palms of their hands turned inward. They were aloof—but glorious.

Her heart did a quick triple beat, like the slide step Ginger Rogers took while dancing the Carioca with Fred Astaire. It occurred to her that the movies were very like life in that everybody truly did have her own story. You wrote your own movie, and you starred in it. One way or another, you made decisions and you stood by them.

With a warm wind tossing her hair, Frankie was at this particular sundown content with her choices.

CHAPTER THREE

In the few minutes it took to drive along Sunset Boulevard, dusk overtook the Model A. Frankie pulled off to the side of the road to park between an old flatbed truck and a battered motorcycle. The swinging green and white sign above a gate in a stucco wall read *Paradise Gardens Villas—No Vacancy*. It was lucky Leo had got them a place here already. Frankie patted the pocket of her coat, where the key lay next to her diamond chip engagement ring. She'd been right to accept the key from Leo—or rather, Connie had been right to insist. And she would find out soon enough what Blanche Carver had meant when she'd said, *You kids will fit in well at Paradise Gardens.*

"Can you smell them? Oranges." Connie leaned out the passenger window.

"You've got a good nose—all I smell are cars. But those are orange trees, all right." She looked up as a grey-and-white dove flew low over the Model A to land atop the high stucco wall beside them. She never would have heard its call had there not been a break in the traffic, but there it was: a soft dove coo that sounded like, *"Who cooks for you? Who cooks for you?"*

They'd been sitting outside Paradise Gardens for less than a minute, but already Frankie was halfway in love with the place. It was so very unlike Vancouver, as different as Marietta Valdes's movie star–red dress was from Frankie's schoolteacher suit. Along this section of Sunset Boulevard, palms and orange trees shadowed the fence, the latter bearing fruit so round and perfect that Frankie thought it prettier than any fruit of the gods could be.

"Who cooks for you?" the dove called again. It seemed that even the birds spoke on cue in Hollywood, for they'd had nothing to eat since cocoa and doughnuts on the road into Los Angeles. The warm evening wind filled Frankie with an electrical excitement that had nothing to do with the painted oranges on her hope chest back in the blue house on Thirty-Sixth Avenue. Or maybe her excitement had everything to do with her hope chest, because that orange crate was a thousand miles distant, and her hopes for today were right here in Hollywood, California.

She said, "I feel like some big hand in the sky has just castled us at chess."

"We castled ourselves," Connie said. "Do you think we're winning?"

"I think we must be. But maybe it's like Blanche Carver said: everybody feels this way when they first arrive in Hollywood." Her stomach growled. Thank goodness there was at least one Newtown apple left to be shared between them. She'd heard it sliding around on the floor of the car as they drove. But when she wiggled herself around the steering wheel to look, there was no apple underneath. The object that had been moving around was King Samson's gun.

She picked up the weapon. She held it in both hands. The two girls stared down at it.

"That gun must like us," Connie said. "It follows us everywhere. Want me to hold on to it?"

"I'll keep it." Frankie slid the gun into her pocket—not the pocket with the key and her engagement ring, but the other, with her one hundred and forty dollars. "One of us can give it back to Samson. Again. If we decide it's advisable."

"It would be kind of an *in* with King Samson, wouldn't it? Giving his gun back to him?"

"If only he weren't such an ungrateful old so-and-so." Frankie pocketed the car key as well. Objects crowded her pockets: keys to the car and a place at Paradise Gardens, lipstick, money, engagement ring. Gun.

"You know what's strange? I was happy just a second ago." Connie sucked her upper lip. "Now I feel a little shy."

"Connie, you weren't even shy on the first day of school. You're probably not even shy right now." Frankie pushed in the clutch. "You're just tired and hungry. And we're all out of apples."

"Think our place will have a kitchen?"

"*Who cooks for us?* We do. At least, we'll soon find out." Frankie climbed down from the driver's seat. "Let's leave our cases stashed in the rumble. I'm sticking to this gun, though. There's nowhere safe to hide it."

"What if I stay with the car while you go and come back and tell me how it is in Paradise Gardens?" But Connie climbed down and slammed the passenger door behind her. She slipped ahead of Frankie through the gate in the stucco wall.

Frankie reached up as she passed beneath the *No Vacancy* sign and slapped it so that it juddered from side to side. She nipped at

Connie's heels along a brick pathway that led between clusters of pink stucco bungalows. How short and friendly were the palms, how pleasing to the eye the dusk-dimmed purples and pinks of the bougainvillea hanging at the windows of the little cottages. She leaned over a low brick edging and ran her hands over the blossoms so that they tickled her palms. Ahead of her, Connie jogged up the path to the door of one of the villas and moved a fan of green leaves aside to reveal the villa's number — 12A. The door flung open, and Connie jumped back out of the way of a bare-chested, laughing young man.

He pulled a blue sweater over his bare torso and loped down the path, followed by a green glass bottle thrown by an unseen hand in the doorway. It smashed against the path, and they all three jumped out of the way.

A woman shouted, "That's the last time you leave me this way, Tom."

Tom tucked his sweater into his slacks and winked at Connie. "I've got to stop dating bearcats and blondes. Or blondes who are bearcats. What are you gals doing, coming or going?"

"Moving in," Frankie said. The broken bottle was followed out of the door by a blue and white plate that flew much better than the bottle had. She ducked. She supposed that she ought to be put off by this first meeting at Paradise Gardens, but instead she felt rather at home. Her father threw things, too — books of sermons mostly, and with no better aim than the unseen blonde, toward whom the youth in the blue sweater was now blowing a kiss. Usually it was because Sheridan D felt he was not receiving adequate respect and consideration from those around him, and she supposed that blondes must sometimes feel the same way. Somewhere nearby, a saxophone wailed. She slipped her hand into her pocket and jingled her ring, gun, money, and key. She pulled the latter out and read the number etched at the top. "We're taking number 7B."

"Villa 7B?" Tom frowned. "Sorry to be the bearer of bad news, dolls, but there are no vacancies at Paradise Gardens. Didn't you see the sign?"

"But we've got the key to 7B," Frankie protested.

In the face of these trim bungalows with their brilliant bougainvillea, sleeping rough in the Model A suddenly appeared to her as intolerable a way to spend their first night in Hollywood as it had earlier seemed to Connie. Her throat grew tight.

"Sorry, kids. If it was up to me, you know?" Tom said. "It cracks a fellow's heart in half to break bad news to a pair of lookers like you."

Frankie shivered. Connie swore. The air had grown cooler as the sunlight became watered with shadow. Frankie slipped her hands into her pockets. She had a sudden wish to pull out King Samson's gun and wave it about, calling, *Sanctuary! I demand sanctuary for two maidens in distress.*

She asked, "If there were an empty place, what kind of rent would they charge?"

"Money's not enough. To live here, you have to be able to …" Tom appeared increasingly uncomfortable. He looked over his shoulder, brows knitting. "Look. Maybe … listen. Like I said, it's not up to me. But do you … ? No."

"*Sure*, we do," Connie said. "Whatever it is you're stammering about, I guarantee we do it."

"Anything!" Frankie agreed. But, thinking of Billie Starr and the Spanish-style brothel, she added, "Well, almost anything."

"And we're pretty smart," Connie said. "Frankie here got an

A in Classical Studies."

"And History," Frankie added, for what it was worth.

"I'm not talking about Greek myths," Tom said. "This isn't about Hercules or Ponce de León. What we know about at Paradise Gardens is movie stars."

"We know lots about movie stars—" Connie began.

Tom interrupted her. "Not what you read in some movie magazine. We want up-to-date items for the news. Blanche Carver owns Paradise Gardens, and gossip is how we pay her our rent."

"No wonder Leo had a key," Connie said.

Frankie added, "So that's what Blanche Carver was talking about when she said we'd really fit in here. She wants gossip, right?"

"You're smoking, kid." Tom nodded. Gossip about movie stars is a business, and we don't reveal our sources to anybody outside Paradise Gardens, even under torture."

"Ha, ha," Connie said.

"I'm as serious as can be. And getting the secrets of the stars is hard labour." Tom raised an eyebrow. "We work days, in the hotels and restaurants where the great ones sleep and eat. And we're extras in their movies. How could new girls like you keep up, straight off the farm?"

"What farm?" Frankie bridled. "Do we look like farm girls to you? We're from Vancouver, Canada." She cast about for an appropriate reference. "Our Dominion Theatre has the biggest neon ceiling in the world, you might like to know."

"Don't take offence. I'm from cow country myself." Tom held out his hands. "But do you sophisticated ladies know any movie stars?"

Connie said, "We certainly do. We know Gilbert Howard, and—"

Tom interrupted her. "*Gilbert Howard?* Cripes, I'm supposed to be over there right now." He hesitated, and then added. "Look, are you on the level about knowing Gilbert Howard?"

Frankie began, "And we know King—"

Connie nudged her, and Frankie stopped mid-sentence. There was no sense spending all they had by way of acquaintance when their mention of Gilbert Howard was still hot in the pot.

Connie said, "We know Gilbert Howard. We've met him twice."

Which they had, if you counted the face in the back window of Marietta Valdes's long Cadillac on the ocean road in Oregon. Frankie added, "He's quite an interesting character."

"Interesting? Gilbert Howard?" Tom laughed. "Maybe you do know him. Come on, then. Follow me. There are still no vacancies at Paradise Gardens, but at least I can give you a taste of Hollywood."

Tom loped along the path, which turned a corner between two bungalows. From behind them, the blonde in Villa 12A shouted out her window, "Good riddance, dames!"

"Want my autograph, blondie?" Connie called back. She exchanged a raised-eyebrow glance with Frankie, and they tore off down the path, following the blue sweater.

Tom led the way around the back of a villa into an overgrown backyard thick with bent grass, smelling of mustard seed, and bounded by a gardenia hedge not much taller than Frankie. With a grunt, he pushed the laurel branches aside with one hand and gestured the girls through with the other. The three crawled deep inside the greenery and peered through at the bungalows next door. The place had something of the air of Paradise Gardens, but there was a more expensive feel to it.

Tom said, "These are the Garden of Allah Villas. Some big names in the movies live here, and there's not even a fence between us and them."

"The Garden of Allah?" Frankie leaned forward to get a better look through the branches. She made out a swimming pool, and cottages grouped around it.

"They have bungalows, like ours, but pricier."

Hollywood architects, Frankie thought, must all admire the Spanish style. Like Paradise Gardens — and like the brothel by the gates to Monument Studios — the Garden of Allah bungalows were roofed in red and stuccoed in white.

She sat in the dry dirt, among the laurel roots and stems, and gazed through the screening leaves at the Garden of Allah. Its swimming pool was lit underwater and glowed like a turquoise jewel. She experienced a moment of envy that vanished when she remembered that her suitcase in the rumble of the Model A didn't contain a bathing suit. The door to one of the white cottages on the far side of the pool opened, and Frankie caught her breath as she recognized Gilbert Howard: tall, lean, and — once again — bare of leg. His hair was perfectly tousled, and his shirt was mis-buttoned down the front.

Gilbert Howard covered a yawn with one hand while the other clasped the shoulder of a fair young man.

The young man stood on Howard's far side, so Frankie couldn't see his face clearly. However, even at that distance, there was no mistaking the look in Gilbert Howard's eyes. Good heavens, Frankie thought. She would never have guessed that Gilbert Howard, the great screen lover, liked men instead of women. But Marietta had spoken truly. Nothing was as it seemed in Hollywood.

Tom pulled a folded blank paper out of his back pocket. He scribbled something, peered out through the bushes, and scribbled again.

Frankie found that her coat was caught on a sharp twig and she shook it free. Something thumped to the ground, and she felt around for it. The gun had fallen from her pocket. She'd have to look for it.

But not now. To improve her view, she pushed leaves and branches to one side. She was rewarded by the sight of Gilbert Howard, that notorious lover of women — on screen and off — leaning down to kiss the fair young man on the lips.

As she watched, the young man unbuttoned his shirt and trousers and dropped both to the ground, revealing not only a complete lack of underwear, but a body unmistakably female, tanned, and lovely. This golden girl turned her back on Howard, sped naked to the lip of the pool, and leapt in.

"Good heavens," Frankie muttered.

At her side, Connie smoothed her skirt across her knees and grinned. "Jumping Jehoshaphat. We certainly are a long way from Vancouver."

"Not so loud," Tom warned. "We're spying, remember. It's no secret that Gilbert Howard likes his females to wear men's clothes."

Connie joked, "When we met Gilbert Howard, he wasn't wearing his trousers then, either. I just thought he was thrifty."

"Somebody ought to tell him men's suits come with a jacket and two pairs of pants," Tom kidded back.

But how funny was it really? Frankie remembered the first girl from the audition, crying her way along Granville Street. She remembered the movie star's boast: *Nobody says no to Gilbert*

Howard. For a handsome man, and with all his charm of manner, Gilbert Howard certainly had an unattractive side. Frankie saw it — even if other girls, like this golden swimmer, did not.

Pencil at the ready, Tom shook his head. "No story here yet, unless some rube somewhere finds skinny-dipping an eye-opener. Still, it's always worth sticking around when Gilbert Howard is living large. You'll see." He wrote something else on the paper, scratched it out, and wrote again. Frankie couldn't make out what he was writing.

Frankie heard the blonde girl call Gilbert Howard's name. The movie star didn't look round. He raised both arms and looked up at the sky. The only word to describe this particular moment, Frankie felt, was *impending.*

"Here we go. See how Howie is standing? He looks like he's on stage, or in front of a camera." Tom shoved paper and pencil back in his pocket. "When Gilbert Howard gets ready to spout Shakespeare …"

"Just a second." Frankie leaned way back and scrabbled among the leaves and stalks. Where in the world had that gun got to?

"Lost something?" Connie asked Frankie.

"Clam up, honey. Watch," Tom said. "If we're lucky, Howie will give us his Hamlet."

Frankie sat back up. *Hamlet,* acted out in front of them by Gilbert Howard? This was no longer spying. This was spectatorship. And spectatorship had a corollary: its audience.

She was Gilbert Howard's hidden audience. Frankie moved a laurel bough aside to get a better view.

At the lip of the pool, Gilbert Howard turned in their direction and lifted his eyes to the heavens, while the naked girl swam the Australian crawl back and forth across the swimming pool. Her golden arms formed arcs above the water, like shining bows lifted again and again in the hunt. Frankie surprised herself by wishing she were as free a young person as this golden girl, willing to dress in a man's clothing and then take said clothing off right in front of everybody.

While the golden girl swam, Gilbert Howard walked along the hedge that hid the three of them. In a voice that seemed to rise up in a wave and spread out across the palms, the roofs, and the hedges around the Garden of Allah, Howard asked, "*What would it pleasure me to have my throat cut with diamonds?*"

"Oh," Frankie breathed. She held one hand tight in the other. She thought, *this is what it feels like when you fall in love.*

"Is that Shakespeare?" Tom asked.

Frankie whispered, "No, it's Webster. *The Duchess of Malfi. Or to be smothered . . .*"

Almost as if he'd heard her, Gilbert Howard called out across the roofs of the Garden of Allah, "*. . . or to be smothered with cassia?*"

"He's the best ham in the business," Tom said. "Premium-quality, smoke-cured bacon."

"Be quiet, will you?" Frankie shook Tom's arm. "This is something. This is . . ."

Gilbert Howard swung his body in a circle, his right heel the fulcrum, and came down hard on his left. His shirt tails swung out like a Scotsman's kilt. He touched his own neck, and in that particular moment she believed in his vulnerability as much as his strength. She believed that somebody would be pleased to cut his throat with diamonds or to smother him with cassia.

She felt privileged to watch him — free of charge. Gilbert Howard might be every woman's downfall, but he was also larger than life. Now that he was acting, he seemed in every way greater than the common man. He was somebody who …

He was *Somebody*. There in the bushes on her first afternoon in Hollywood, Frankie decided that she wanted to be Somebody, too. How did you get to be larger than everyday life, though? How did you get to be Somebody?

Was Gilbert Howard born that way? Perhaps a regular person like Frankie, a substitute schoolteacher who only dreamed of acting in the movies, could never be what Gilbert Howard was. Perhaps you needed to be born under a special star, or sired by Zeus, or constructed from very special family attributes that show up early and mean you are destined for greatness.

So much did she desire to be like Gilbert Howard that she nearly howled with frustration. She put both hands over her mouth to keep herself quiet. At the side of the pool, Gilbert Howard avoided a splash from the naked girl in the water by taking two steps closer to the hedge that hid Tom, Connie, and Frankie.

Frankie pulled back deeper into the bushes.

Gilbert Howard raised his fists and shook them at the stars. *"What would it pleasure me to be shot with pearls?"*

Tom muttered, "I'd pay money to see this. Luckily, it's a free show, like his skinny-dipping girlfriend there." Tom took a flask out of his pocket, uncapped it, and offered it to Frankie. She was thinking of accepting when the branches over their heads rattled and parted. A diamond of sky framed Gilbert Howard's face. He gazed down at the three of them.

Swift movement at her side told Frankie that Tom was tucking his pencil and paper out of sight. "Now we're in for it," he muttered. "He hates it when we spy."

But Gilbert Howard only said, "Young women in the bushes, coo-ee!" He held out his hand to Tom. Tom handed over his flask.

Gilbert Howard took a swig. He eyed Frankie. "I know you, don't I?"

Frankie took a deep breath. "Sure, Mr Howard. I'm—"

"Don't tell me." Howard took another swig from Tom's flask. "I don't want to know your name. You'll just be the brunette in the hedgerow, and that's special, isn't it? Thanks for the refreshment, Tom."

Connie began to struggle to her feet. "Hi, Howie. Do you remember me?"

"Sit down, honey," Howard said. He hardly glanced at her. "Sit down before my swimming sweetheart over in the pool sees what you do to me. Say, what the hell is *cassia?* Does anybody know?"

"Cassia is a kind of yellow flower," Frankie told the actor.

Gilbert Howard guffawed. "If you're going to say something so wantonly intelligent, at least have the decency to wear glasses." The movie star leaned down and patted the crown of Frankie's head. "You know, you've got something, and I think it's a creeping cleverness. But brains are no use in the movies. *I* know, because I used to teach school long ago, in my first youth. Talent's the thing. Talent and hard work, damn it all. But if they don't help, brains won't hold you back, either, so take heart."

Gilbert Howard had been a schoolteacher. Just like Frankie.

With a journalist's aplomb, Tom asked, "Say, what's it like to be at the top, Mr Howard?"

"It's like the top of anything, isn't it?" Gilbert Howard's smile deserted him for a moment. "There's only one way from here."

He took another slug from Tom's flask, tucked the flask into his pocket, and walked away.

"Gilbert Howard doesn't remember me," Connie whispered. "It was only a few days ago, but he doesn't remember."

Frankie hardly heard her. She was too engaged in watching the movie star turn his back and walk, barelegged, barefooted, and a little stooped about the shoulders, across the pool toward one of the villas. He might be Somebody now, but Gilbert Howard had once been a regular fellow. And so must the so-called gods and goddesses of Hollywood have started out as everyday people. They had talent, looks, and luck, but they were all human — Greta Garbo, Clark Gable, even Marietta Valdes — just like Frankie.

"I could be a movie star," Frankie told Tom. "I've said it before, but I didn't believe it. I thought you had to shine, to have *something* — like you, Connie — in order to be more than just a bit actress. But now I see that if I'm good enough, and if I'm lucky, then I can shine, too. Like Gilbert Howard. And like Marietta Valdes."

"How come he didn't remember me?" Connie asked. "Men always remember me."

Tom said, "Maybe he'll remember you next time. Say, when you're big stars, girls, do me a favour. Get my flask back from Gilbert Howard, will you?"

Frankie felt the joy of unlimited possibility travel through her like cold water on a hot day. She looped her arms around Connie's neck and Tom's. "I've got a hundred and forty dollars," she said, which was more than she meant to tell a stranger, but this was one of those moments where anything went. "I'll buy you a new flask."

"You're the gnat's elbow, kiddo. And that was the best quote I've ever collected from Gilbert Howard, thanks to you two. *There's only one way from the top.*" Tom fought his way out of the hedge, and Frankie followed. "I'm going to tell the Queen about you."

"What Queen?" On hands and knees, Frankie followed Tom the last few feet out of the laurels. It felt good to stand up, and she stretched her arms over her head.

"The Queen of the Extras."

Connie said, "You know, between Gilbert Howard and King Samson, I'm starting to feel like a broken blossom."

"Come on, petal. You've still got that something, and we've only been in Hollywood a couple of hours. It's too soon to give in to despair." Frankie dusted leaves and bits of grass out of every fold and corner on her person. She held out her hand and pulled her friend to her feet. Behind them, the Garden of Allah held its collection of big shots. Before them stood the back doors of several Paradise Gardens bungalows, cheap and cheerful, but just as much a part of Hollywood.

"Where's the music coming from?"

In the distance, she heard the opening notes of 'Dora Heart'.

Tom sang, "*Hey de ho de hee …*"

Connie answered, "*Hi de hee de hi …*"

Frankie ducked around a little orange tree behind the nearest villa, thinking that 'Dora Heart' was like the moon. No matter how many miles she travelled, there it was. Then again, maybe all great songs were like the moon.

Frankie dodged a string of Christmas lights hung a little too low from a villa window, noting as she passed that the lights were made in the shape of parrots: red and green, yellow and blue, the connections loose and sparking. She remembered the gun she'd left in the bushes between Paradise Gardens and the Garden of Allah and turned back the way they'd come.

Tom caught her by the arm. "You girls like to dance a conga?"

Frankie knew she ought to turn back and search for that gun again, but she told herself it was too dark to find anything in those bushes. Anyway, nobody else had seen the gun. It was perfectly safe to leave it there until morning.

With a feeling between her shoulder blades that should have been caution but instead felt like excitement, Frankie followed Connie into a crowded, open courtyard. They arrived at the centre of Paradise Gardens just in time to see the sun set with a final flash of light through the slatted branches of a palm tree.

DREAM HYPNOSIS

Matthew Walsh

Matthew Walsh is a queer writer from Nova Scotia whose debut poetry book was published with Goose Lane Editions. Their new work can be seen in Applebeard Editions's new anthology and the Bad Nudes anthology, as well as Pulp Literature Issue 10, Summer 2016.

Dream Hypnosis

Maybe it would be nice to be hypnotized
by my dreams. They are little dreams

where I want to read a poem for you in
my crab voice though you hate astrology.

It is from a book I bought while a little
tipsy the other night and the words were

simply bubbles from my ocean mouth &
I had tried saving my own poem on my phone.

I could not be hypnotized once in Slave Lake
though my eyes were veils, black and white.

I have to take care of my feet and buy them
a brand-new loofah the colour of clown hair.

I identify wholeheartedly with the fool, their
esoteric system of dreams and interpretations.

& my literal dream where I have a hard shell
because I am a crab-human with concerns.

They are little dreams where you find crab-me,
& put me in an ice cream bucket type Vancouver condo

with a rotary phone which I cannot dial out on
because I have pincers & there is no phone

usage tutorial in crab. They are little dreams where I say *how
European* to the artless walls in my crab voice but I do not

understand anything and to you it seems like I accept
this setting which is a dream I see with my televised eyes,

where I meet a Kenoran & tell them about blue crabs of Kenora
to find out no blue crabs exist in Kenora and they must be dreamed.

Dreams when I just go hmmmmm and plant potatoes
all day after I drink passionately from the rain barrel.

Dreams when my phone died
and I wanted to take a shower and your call

went to my voicemail eventually. Dreams
when I say *Okay. Okay. Okay. Was he? Why?*

Okay. Dreams when you say I am a patient and I say
Ahhhhhhhhhhhh. Yep. Where I take inventory

of general stuff in my ice cream bucket. Dreams where I need
a couple Lamborghinis and I'm a stud finder.

I still have to deal with that. Sounds like I need to pare back,
yet still master communicating in my perfect bubble

language. Where I remember the heat of a long-ago potato
shed & how you sucked the cold from my tongue.

A PARABLE OF THINGS THAT CRAWL AND FLY

Graham Robert Scott
and Wallace Cleaves

Graham Robert Scott is an English professor at Texas Woman's University, where he teaches writing and the occasional speculative fiction literature class. His stories have appeared in Nature, Barrelhouse, and X-R-A-Y Literary Mag. He has been collaborating with Wallace Cleaves on academic and creative projects for decades, and they are already at work on a new story.

Wallace Cleaves is Associate Professor of Teaching and Associate Director in the University Writing Program at the University of California at Riverside. He also teaches courses in medieval, Renaissance, and Native American literature. He is a member of the Tongva (also known as Gabrieleno) Native American community.

$\mathcal{A}$ Parable of Things that Crawl and Fly

Every hour, every minute, I hear the throaty, chuckling call of a raven. Sometimes He makes a showing. On the afternoon our unexpected visitors arrived, He appeared and gave me a disapproving look with one eye. I read the look as *You should be working, Helen.* I gave Him side-eye: *Even the turtles rest, Raven.* I'd been on break for two minutes.

Far beyond Raven, past rows of unnaturally aligned palm trees, a plume of dust appeared on the road, the signature of a distant oncoming car foregrounded against foothills of umber and sienna. Neither Gabe nor I said anything about the approaching vehicle, though cars rarely came this way. Instead, Gabe tilted his spotted, bristly head toward me, slid a toothpick from one side of the mouth to the other, and flashed me a grin so I'd know a joke was coming.

"Met this guy, oh, would have been eleven years ago." Gabe's voice, a rich, dark timbre from a lifetime of smoking, has always reminded me of cracked leather. Thanks to a lifetime of field work, his skin did, too. "I was nursing a railway lager in this desert bar called Mama Jane's — one of those places with pickups out front and semis clumped like Tetris blocks out back — and this dude drags himself onto the stool beside me. Bone tired. Eyes deep-seated. Hollow. Complexion, hair, facial structure of a full-blooded indigenous man. Which may have, I admit, prompted an involuntary snort on my part."

I said nothing at this. I'm not always nice to *reconstitines* either. It's not their fault, of course. Not anyone's fault, really. Once folks realized they could swap out of their children's DNA any trace of the white folks who had raped their way into the family tree, anyone who wasn't an asshole thought that made good sense. But like other customs born of good intentions, the *reconstitine* practice got a bit carried away. Some faces have social capital. In time, families who had been white for generations, with no tribal affiliations or knowledge of Native cultures, were having kids who looked pre-Columbian. If it came down to splitting hairs, my problem wasn't so much with the kids; my problem was with what they represented. But on my face, in the tone of my voice, it came out a lot like I didn't like them, and I had long ago stopped apologizing for it.

"Of course, he heard me," Gabe said, "so I felt obligated to apologize — "

Wuss.

" — and when he was cool about the whole thing, I felt maybe I owed him a conversation."

Grandmaster wuss.

The car came to a stop in the middle of the road for no apparent reason. I wondered whether someone was fiddling with directions, having an argument, necking in the backseat, taking a nap. Dust in the car's wake settled onto tree branches, created plumes of spinning motes in waning sunlight.

"Turns out, my new friend was tired on account of a sick kid. Which, of course, meant now I had to ask about his boy. And *that's* how I learned that, when he and his wife — also reconstituted — named their son, they wanted to use authentic Native American naming practices."

"Oh, God," I said.

"You know, those descriptive names. Drinks from Bottle. Eats with Ketchup. Fills a Diaper."

Gabe knows this sort of thing makes me mutter. I'm only an eighth Tongva, but I'm a documented member of the tribe. Focused my whole life studying our culture. Three books. A career of public lectures and one film documentary. Thirty peer-reviewed articles. In the back room of the house, eleven cryocasks with minds bequeathed to my one-woman institute by passing elders. When I wasn't listening to Gabe or the Raven, I listened to the minds, almost eleven hours a day. Tried to provoke memories with auditory, visual, olfactory cues. Tried to find evidence of what we used to be while it still existed. For decades, I'd been driven by the sense that I owed that to the relatives who once lived and thrived here. But even with the caskets and the minds in them, the work was hard. Memories deteriorated. Became closed off, inaccessible, harder to provoke. Turned out it was easier to summon up the faces of the past than to conjure their stories.

In the distance, the car started up again.

"This didn't really happen, Gabe," I said.

He gave me a look, daring me to contradict his tale. Then he continued. "Guess what they named their first son."

Ugh. "Stands with DNA?"

"Only Child."

He paused and waited, casual as the sun stretching its rays.

"They named their *first* son Only Child," I clarified.

His grin revealed teeth. Right. *Reconstitine* couples sometimes needed pointers on birth control.

"Fine, I'll bite. What did they name their *second* son?"

"Last Child."

I choked on my tea. "Sounds like only one of those was accurate."

"Oh, hell," Gabe said. "Neither was. Third time around, they said *fuck it* and named her Sarah."

As the car hummed into the driveway of our farm and slid to a stop on a blanket of leaves, Raven — who had not moved this entire time — let out a throaty warble.

Gabe ignored the bird or didn't hear Him. Instead, he gestured at the car. "Speaking of *reconstitines*."

Having guessed who was coming from far off, Gabe had picked his story for the occasion. My son-in-law Yurok sat in what would have once been a driver's seat. Reconstituted Native features resembling neither of his parents. Name from the wrong tribe. Hair, showing touches now of grey, braided into a fashionable tail that someone with a similar complexion probably told him was authentic. Gloria wasn't with him. I tried to remember the last time I'd smelled my daughter's hair, hugged her, seen her smile at me. When I realized it was going to take a depressing amount of rummaging to find that memory, I gave up.

Then Yurok reached into the back. To the child seat there, with my granddaughter in it. All thirteen months of her, brown as my great-grandma, fidgeting and squirming and impatient to escape her prison of straps. My heart, not expecting her to be aboard, went dizzy. There's a kind of nappy contentment that takes over when you hold your baby or grandchild, and all of the perils of the world take on soft, fuzzy edges. A gentle, humming, oxytocin buzz. I was already feeling it, and she was still in the car.

It was smart of him, bringing her.

The Tongva creation story we like to tell our children has several versions. One goes like this:

Long, long ago, there was only the endless sea below and the sentient Sky above.

All of that sameness in all directions seemed wrong to the Sky.

One day, however, the Sky discovered seven bumps in the great ocean, and He liked the way each broke the monotony. He brought his great face closer to see them better. Seven bumps, far apart. Seven bumps, and sometimes they moved. Seven bumps, each one the shell of an enormous turtle, rising high above the water.

The Sky spoke to the turtles, then, saying, "Gather here, for I have need of you."

Obedient creatures, the turtles gathered beneath his face. Easily exhausted creatures, they fell into a deep sleep, resting on the waves.

The Sky didn't mind. Their sleep served His purpose well. He reached down into the ocean, plunging His hands through the surface of the sea. As the Sky's forearms pierced the ocean, He impregnated the waters with an abundance of life. Fish and swimming things of all varieties came into being. Deeper and deeper the Sky's arms plunged. And when His hands reached the bottom of the sea, He kept pushing, through the muck and slime, the sand and rock that lies below. In so doing, He generated all the crawling and wriggling things that live on the ocean floor.

Now, with His hands deep into the rock, the Sky heaved up huge mountains of earth from the heart of the world, wreaking terrible violence to sea and earth, but spawning more living things wherever He touched. Once the Sky had enough earth, He heaped it on the backs of the seven sleeping turtles. He lumped rocks together to craft mountains. He scooped out hollows to carve valleys.

All the world we know exists on the backs of those turtles, which live still, pinned to the ocean floor under the obscene weight piled upon them by the Sky.

After Yurok paid the car and it hummed down the road, I kept him at bay, doing grandmotherly things. I listened to Temecula burble about something she saw on the drive over, made her a sandwich, brought her juice and a cookie. I called her *Topangna*, a proper Tongva name, which made her giggle and her father frown.

"She had snacks on the road," Yurok protested, hovering, clearly wanting to talk about whatever he came to talk about. Which would almost certainly cost me time or money.

I helped Temecula eat, listened to her some more, cooed at her, cleaned her up, then laid her on the table to check her diaper. I found it light, unencumbered, pristine. Then I remembered Yurok's car stopping on the road and realized he'd stopped to change her before arriving, anticipating I would check.

Out of spite, I changed her diaper anyway, and behind me, I heard Yurok sigh. Temecula gave me a puzzled look until she heard Raven calling outside and started looking through the window for Him.

After, I bounced her on my lap for a spell, feeling her fist grip my index finger. She burbled some more at me. I regretted not having a Rosetta Stone to decipher it all. That was often my difficulty, translating my relations. Always too young, or too dead.

"Maybe we should set her up with the TV," Yurok said.

Gabe shuffled through with a beer he'd plucked from an Igloo on the porch. "Gave it away," he said. And he plopped, cross-legged on the floor.

Temecula reached out toward Gabe and made grasping motions. "'Abe!"

Reluctantly, I let her run to him, and my defence was gone. As Yurok visibly psyched himself up to talk to me about whatever he'd come for, my blood pressure swelled and neck muscles tightened. I hate confrontation—enough that I moved to the middle of nowhere, enough that I bristle and fume pre-emptively when anyone corners me. And so, as Gabe walked Temecula to the living room, I closed my eyes, imagined ocean waves lapping at the coast. I could hear Gabe whispering to a captivated Temecula our creation story, and I wondered just how much she understood beyond "turtles." Whenever I hear Gabe tell his version, I become transported. Hear the murmuring of the sea. See the water spread out to eternity on all sides far below me. And while there, looking down on the great sea from the vault of heaven, my perspective is cosmic and wise and eternal.

Then the Raven trilled and the ocean was gone.

"How's the research going?" Yurok asked.

Yurok was learning subtleties. I hadn't expected him to lead with that kind of question. Feeling no obligation to return the favour, I hit him with everything. Gave him the tour. Georgina Hidalgo's mind was the oldest of the lot. It was so far gone that I could spend a whole day in there and not learn a thing. Little coherent, anyway. Mand Hurley's mind had newer memories, much more vivid, but also far less useful because he was the youngest. Still, sometimes he'd seen or overheard something that was still in there, ready to be quickened and relived. Our nine other minds formed a kind of spectrum between those two. I told Yurok about the (slowly) accumulating cognitive, archaeological, and linguistic evidence that coastal Tongvas might have admixed with Polynesians long ago. How our names and designs for *tomolo* sewn-plank boats and composite bone hooks were similar to those of early Hawaiians. How clues of that connection were vanishing whenever we lost an elder.

It was about that point I recognized his disappointed expression, thinly concealed. He hadn't asked about my research out of curiosity. He was inquiring about my availability. And I'd just made it clear I was nowhere near done with my life's work. Nowhere near done speaking for the dead.

"Okay, what is it?" I asked.

"We took on more care debt this year," he said, slow and flat. This was peak Yurok. Near the beginning of a conversation, his voice affected the rhythmic cadence of Native slow-talking, as though he'd consciously assembled his speaking style as a pastiche of old movie tropes. I'd never met anyone from the old reservations who talked that way except when showing off for tourists. I doubted he had either. His speech accelerated whenever he forgot himself.

"I see," I said. Not much else to say. This was perhaps the third or fourth year their young family was unable to keep up with payments on mandated health insurance, forced to borrow from the same government that created the requirement.

"That debt grew about eight percent this year."

Sigh. Maybe if he tried his hand at something other than waiting tables and unpaid internships? "You need money." At least, I hoped that was it. At my age, money is cheaper than time.

"No. Christ, no."

"Sounds like you do."

He ran fingers through his hair, up to the crown. "That isn't why I came here."

Why *he* came here. *He.* "Where's Gloria?"

Yurok looked at his shoes, a pair of ratty loafers: "Working, always working. Trying to get ahead of the curve, you know."

"That makes sense. Why aren't you working, too?"

Yurok sighed, fidgeted now with his ponytail, tugged on a sleeve is if to correct some wrinkle. The man was always fiddling about, as though he didn't quite feel comfortable in anything he was wearing, even himself. "I'm not——"

"——contributing?"

"Lazy," he said. "I'm not lazy."

And at that, he left the room, having never reached his point.

Gloria answered, first ring. We spent a few minutes faking our way through pleasantries before she asked what happened and I told her.

"He has jobs, Mom. Like everyone else our age," she said, by which she meant thirty-eight. "He has several."

"Not real jobs."

"There are no real jobs. Not anymore. Just gigs and so-called opportunities," she said. "You get a cheap retail or service job to cover health insurance, if you can find one. But if you want to advance, get job security or personal fulfilment or whatever, then you have to build clout, build audience. So you juggle gigs for exposure. They pay crap, or, more likely, nothing at all. Or you go to school, or into training, and pay to work while racking up student debt. On top of that, you maybe find something else that pays well, but without exposure or insurance. Like crime."

"Gloria!"

"I'm kidding, Mom," she said, though maybe she wasn't. I couldn't tell anymore with her.

"I know plenty of people with real, full-time jobs," I said. "Sure you're looking hard enough?"

Her laugh was fast, penetrating, like a gunshot.

A second later, she mumbled an apology, then asked, "How old are those people you know? On average?"

My crowd skews septuagenarian. Blame selection bias. "I know what you're going to say, Gloria. And yeah, sure, they're old enough to have paid their dues. But you'll get your turn. I know lots of people who went through the entry-level stuff you're dealing with. Mostly in the arts, or academia. And they got through it. Everything turned out okay."

"The average age of a Fortune 500 executive right now is ninety-two. The *average*."

"Is that right?" I hadn't kept up on that kind of thing.

"The average age of a stratoclass citizen is a hundred-and-three."

"Point being?"

"They're not retiring, Mom. They're not even dying. And all the new jobs that trickle down are cheap, flimsy, transitory things. It's a lot worse downhill than you think it is."

"Downhill?"

"Talk to Yurok."

"You're doing a better job than he was, honey."

"Yeah, well, he has a big ask. One that would be rude coming from me."

"But not from him?"

"You've made it clear he's inauthentic, an outsider. So no, Mom, the rules are different for him. Please hear him out?"

With Gabe asleep on the couch and Temecula out cold on his chest, I found Yurok by following the reverberating shots from Gabe's old AR-15.

Months earlier, Gabe had poured ordnance gelatine into five old coffee cans. These now bristled with spiky holes, propped on a series of posts before a field of black sage and yucca several thousand feet deep, ending in a low ridgeline that once sprouted trees. Sighting down the top of the rifle, butt tucked into his shoulder, Yurok hammered the cans methodically, *pow*, pause, *pow*, pause, *pow*. I realized I often heard this same pattern in the minutes following our confrontations, and for a moment, instead of speaking, I peered at the distant cans, looking for any drawings resembling a face.

"I called a car," he said, not looking my way. "Just waiting for it to show."

"I called Gloria," I echoed. "She said I should try again."

He sighed, lowered his sight a nudge, and then raised it again. *Pow.*

"Well," I tried again. "I'm here. What do you need, Yurok?"

"No point," *Pow.* "We both know your answer."

"Maybe. But I promise I'll listen."

"Yeah?"

"I just said so."

"Okay, then," he began, and without relenting in his barrage except to reload, Yurok paid me back for my lecture about the heads and Polynesians. He rattled off statistics on income, declining birth rates, bimodal life expectancies, bimodal socio-economic distribution, student debt, care debt, job creation (mostly in service and retail), job compression (mostly in the fields anyone would want), job gigification, and average cost of health care by year of life. In a biting, clipped voice punctuated by gunshots, he insisted the system continued to depend on and assume a middle class that no longer existed, *pow*, except for a few people in transition, heading up, *pow*, or heading down, *pow*. That nowhere was the problem more severe than in fucking health care, where, once you boiled the whole thing down, *pow*, tracked dollars from pockets to payouts, the dwindling supply of young folk were being forced to pay for additional years of life for the growing elderly elite, *pow*, each year of additional life for those entitled geezers more expensive than the last, *pow*, all with the reassurance that the young would eventually work themselves out *pow* of *pow* the *pow* hole, *pow*. Yet how could that happen when the ancient goddamned stratoclass refused to retire, refused to die, refused to hire, except in fucking gigs and drabs, *pow*? Oh, sure they were told that in the old days, people started their own companies, *pow*, but had Helen, *pow*, looked at the licensing and fees and start-up requirements lately, *pow*? That door closed on new folk long ago. Only people who were likely to pull that kind of thing off were the very fucking people, the fucking rich people, who didn't need it, *pow*. Who even today were still unlikely to be any kind of indigenous, *reconstitine* or otherwise, *pow*. And you can reassure the young at the base of the pyramid they'll someday be at the top, but now that the entire economy is, in fact, a pyramid scheme with dollars borrowed at the bottom to pay elites at the top, most of them are dying of stress long before they ever climb above those lower steps. *Pow pow pow.*

By which point, Yurok was no longer slow-talking.

I didn't have much to say to all that. I wasn't stratoclass. Far from it. But according to his numbers, I was part of a vanishingly small, obsolete upper-middle, making assumptions about the rest of the economy that were more historical than topical. Maybe I'd been a bit myopic. I remembered the trends of my youth, the adjunctification of academia and evaporating pay for artists. It's easy to fool yourself into thinking those things have stopped, or had been exaggerated in your youth, once you're no longer subject to them.

"Assuming that's all true," I began, "what do you need from me?"

"Next year's an even number," Yurok said. "I'm running for Congress."

"Well, good for you," I said.

"We've done the research. Lots of it. My chance of winning borders on zero," he added. "Unless I can get my clout up to around two-sigma."

Two-sigma. My own clout score. I wasn't a Noam Chomsky, but I was up there. My stomach ached, started rolling like it was looking for an exit. "You need my endorsement," I said, hoping that was the extent of it.

Yurok just looked at me and waited.

No, of course not. He needed enough of a rep to draw money and votes, enough to unseat an incumbent. In a year. An endorsement alone wouldn't cut it.

"Dammit, Yurok," I said. "Out with it."

"You're sitting out here telling the stories of the dead," he said. "And I get how important that is. But you're worried about losing who the Tongva were, while the Tongva who are left *are dying now*. You're losing the stories of the living. And people need to hear them if anything's going to change."

"Someone else can tell those stories."

"No, Helen, they can't," Yurok said. "Might have been true long ago, when the playing field was level. But talk to any of our aspiring voices today. They're all stuck in the minor leagues, scrabbling for readers and viewers one unpaid gig or academic hoop at a time, hoping to get noticed and relevant before they die. Most won't be. Not when there are three-sigmas out there who have been doing their thing for more than half a century, and who gatekeep nearly every channel of communication. All I have right now is you. If I run, and you document what I'm doing, why I'm doing it, how I'm representing a whole people affected by this crap, maybe we can shake things up a little."

I dwelled on this for a minute. Yurok let me. He disassembled the rifle on a blanketed picnic table, began cleaning the buffer assembly and spring.

"You know, even if I do this, you're probably not going to win," I observed.

"Doesn't matter."

"I don't follow."

"I don't need to win. I need to do so well that they can't ignore what we're saying."

"Yurok," I said, and when he looked up at me, I could see he already knew. Already knew the price. But I said it anyway.

"Every hour I spend on this is an hour of data lost forever. I already feel guilty just spending time on this conversation. I feel guilty when I sleep."

He said nothing.

I continued, "Those are people I knew, people who trusted me. Elders. Do you get how deep respect of elders goes in our culture? If I do this, I'm pissing away what they gave me. And those weren't easy asks."

"Neither is this."

Raven was perched on the eaves of the house, cocking a head to peer one eye at me. Omens of change are notoriously tough to interpret. They might signal the end of anything. A life, an era. The bird, useless, said nothing.

I went back inside.

The story goes that, one day, the turtles woke up. The first to rouse stretched his neck, kinked from supporting the island that rested upon it, and that island moved miles farther away from the others. Then another awakened and crawled to colder waters to chill the ache in his shell, which had grown sore from supporting a mountain range. The ripples of his passing woke another turtle who sought balmy waters to the south to ease his burden. As the turtles scraped along the seafloor, the land that rested on their backs shook and trembled. Mountains tumbled. Rifts opened in the spaces between the turtle's shells.

In time, the turtles tired again, and fell back asleep. They were, after all, quite literally bearing the weight of the world upon their shells.

And so the cycle goes.

When the turtles awaken, volcanoes roar and the world shudders.

When the turtles fall into exhausted slumber, those who live on their backs fool themselves into thinking the world will always be this way.

I'm in the kitchen now, making *wiiwish*, acorn mush. The ritual of shelling, grinding, and leaching acorns always soothes. Better than yoga. More productive too. It isn't even that bitter anymore. Selection and genetic modification have resulted in a hearty, drought-happy version of *quercus agrifolia* light enough in tannin to be pleasant on the palate. Not everything new is a bad thing.

Temecula, awake again, waddles outside to her father, who has stowed Gabe's rifle. It occurs to me she's part of Yurok's argument. A reminder of higher stakes down the road. Down the hall from the kitchen and through the open door of my study, the cryocask status indicators blink blue and white, and overlapping shadows race as the screensaver plays across the walls. Normally reassuring, the lights now strike me as impatient, like the ticking of a clock.

Outside, Raven ruffles feathers, and the Moon gleams.

In Tongva tales, the first person to live on the back of the cosmic turtles was a man named Weywot. In some versions of his story, Weywot is an innocent, betrayed by sons impatient to rule the people themselves. In the versions I like the most, he's a cruel tyrant, and his sons poison him with his own feces. They free themselves from tyranny only by inventing mortality. Weywot never goes entirely away. Coyote tears out his heart as it lies on the funeral pyre and throws it into the Sky. There, his heart becomes the Moon, a reminder in our darkest moments that all things wax and wane, that nothing is eternal, but perhaps, also, that nothing is ever fully lost either.

Looking up at that reminder tonight, though, I don't know. I feel like the knowledge donated to me can only wane.

Mand Hurley knew another version of our Weywot story, one I hadn't heard before gleaning it from his mind. In Hurley's telling, Weywot teaches his people that change is coming in the form of death. That they must give way to new generations, who will inherit the world from them. That though they may never understand why, things will always change. The people fear this news so much that they turn on Weywot and kill him, whereupon everything changes anyway.

The Sky is almost black now. The Moon is quiet, having stopped beating long ago. Flickering blue and white lights beckon from down the hall. Waiting. Ticking. Drumming spectral fingers. In the other room, Temecula squeals with joy at Gabe's clowning.

Behind it all, I hear again, insistent, the throaty call of the Raven. Speaking of change, speaking of death, perhaps of both.

HANDS

Rebecca Ruth Gould

Rebecca Ruth Gould *is the author of the poetry collection* Cityscapes *(Alien Buddha Press, 2019) and the award-winning monograph* Writers & Rebels *(Yale University Press). She has translated many books from Persian and Georgian, including* After Tomorrow the Days Disappear: Ghazals and Other Poems of Hasan Sijzi of Delhi *(Northwestern University Press, 2016) and* The Death of Bagrat Zakharych and other Stories *by Vazha-Pshavela (Paper & Ink, 2019). A Pushcart Prize nominee, she was a finalist for the Luminaire Award for Best Poetry (2017) and for Lunch Ticket's Gabo Prize (2017).*

Hands

What struck her most about him were his hands. They were long and lanky, like his body. Even more remarkable than their shape was the way he used them. When they first met, he shook her hands boldly and directly, as if it were a perfectly normal thing to do and not a violation of the law in the Islamic Republic of Iran. Taken aback, she forgot to respond. Her hand hung limply in his palm until he dislodged it.

Just the day prior, she had read about a poet who, after returning from abroad, had been arrested for shaking a woman's hand. She wanted to warn him: *You shouldn't do that. You might end up in jail for shaking my hands.* But he must have known what he was doing, she reasoned, and who was she to tell him how to behave in his own country?

His hands didn't fit anywhere, not in his pockets or at his sides. They dangled oddly from his arms, like an expert swimmer more at home in a lake than on dry land. The lines on his palms were long, stretching from his wrist to his index fingers. If a fortune-teller—like the one she had just consulted with in Hafez's tomb in Shiraz—had been asked to read his palms, she would have predicted for him a long life, a fulfilling marriage, and many children. His hands were like an autonomous body. She imagined them keeping her warm at night, soothing the aches in her back, providing a resting ground for her lips, caressing her hips.

Before they said goodbye that magical night in Tehran, she asked him why he'd decided to shake her hand. Without answer, he waxed lyrical in a different direction. "I dream of working wonders with my hands," he said. "I want to become a perfumist. I want to make magic potions and aphrodisiacs based on ancient Iranian traditions." Although it was not an answer, it opened a new mysterious horizon onto his soul. She wanted to know more.

She touched his hands again in Tbilisi, where they had arranged to rendezvous in order to get to know each other better. There in the Georgian Republic, they could say things — about politics and to each other — that could not be said so long as they were within the confines of the Islamic Republic. They could hold hands publicly without breaking the law. Funny, she thought, how law interacts with morality, indeed with honesty: what is licit in one country is suddenly an offence when the jurisdiction shifts. Strange how acts of affection, expressions of love, can be made a crime. Her hands pressed hard on his body. Certain parts of him yielded in certain ways, though not every crevice and not in every way. Her hands traced a continual arc on his back while they worked together, stimulating the flow of words, summoning and cementing memory.

She saw his hands again in Abu Dhabi, but this time it was different. She was cautious. She wanted to see what his hands would do with her body when unprompted. Nearly all of their contact had been initiated by her hands in Tbilisi. This time, she decided, she would let his fingers determine their movements, would wait for his nails to dig into her skin and his thumbs to press into the small of her back. While she waited for him to touch her, she remembered when he shook her hands unbidden, in full public view, in violation of the law, in Tehran. Looking back on that moment, she wondered whether she had misread his apparent courage. Was it perhaps a performance, not for her sake but for the state, an act of civil disobedience that dared the government to punish him? *Hospitality demands that we shake the hand of every guest,* his handshake seemed to say in retrospect, as he failed to touch her now that they were alone at last. *We must pay our respects to every visitor!* Or was she demeaning that miraculous moment? What force of gravity had caused him to extend his hand then and withdraw it now?

Now that they were alone together for the second time in Abu Dhabi, his hands were more reticent than she had ever seen them in Tehran or Tbilisi. It was as if they belonged in another place, on another body, or in another galaxy. She decided she would wait until they said goodbye to question why his hands appeared to be tied down by a psychic force she could not fathom, and why they were so hesitant to touch her body. And then, in the airport, there was a crush of people, as there always is. The lines extended out into the arrivals hall as the boarding time approached. Five thirty. Five thirty-five. The day was just beginning, yet it felt like the end of time. *All passengers for Tehran, please approach gate 6D,* the intercom blared. The moment to speak had passed — she had to touch his hands. She reached out to find them, but they were tugged deep inside his pockets, too deep for her to reach.

The endless deferral of discussion, along with his unreachable hands that could have brought words to his lips, prevented them from broaching the most pressing issue: when would their hands meet again? He asked her to watch his luggage while he went to the bathroom. When he returned, he had to rush to catch his flight. There was no time to say goodbye, no time to repeat the gestures that brought them together in Tehran and Tbilisi, no time for her to take the measure of his hands, to impress his knuckles on her memory, to lift his fingertips to her lips, and to tell him how much she wanted his hands — but actually the entirety of his body and of his soul — in her life. Perhaps, she decided, the crush of people was the best way of deferring this impossible speech. Maybe silence was the preferred option. Not knowing what to say in the little time remaining to them, she closed her eyes and imagined his fingers stroking her hair. When she opened her eyes, he was gone.

A TREE SLOWLY ROTS

David Troupes

David Troupes has published two full collections of poetry, Parsimony *(2009) and* The Simple Men *(2012), and his work has appeared in many journals on both sides of the* Atlantic, including Hayden's Ferry Review, Fugue, Nimrod, PN Review, Alaska Quarterly Review, Northern New England Review, Poetry Wales, *and Carcanet's 2015 anthology* New Poetries VI. *Having recently completed a PhD and a Jerwood Opera Writing Fellowship in the UK, he is happily planning a return to his native Massachusetts.*

A Tree Slowly Rots

i

Autumn in the sculleries —
dusk tubs and heat pipes,
crows smoking moonwards through an afterglow of west

and I wander like a guest
in the evening of a grand house, crumbling, hearing music, rumours,
     vague steps.
Let the lord forget me. My own home is a hated place.

ii

No more, you say. No more
of hills and crows. Something older. Some form
snoring at the ankles. Tell us. Some first earth

crashing in its spin. Tell us of the wolf breath
whisky fume of the living room,
the body on the floor.

BUDDHA IN A BOTTLE

Susan Pieters

Susan Pieters, one of the founding forces at Pulp Literature, *is now an actual Vancouver resident instead of just a virtually-in-Vancouver-but-really-in-Burnaby-where-it's-cheaper resident. Yep, now she's squeezed herself into a smaller square footage, hence the inspiration for this story. She's still unpacking boxes, but Sue promises that she'll get her website up by the time you read this, really she will! Try her at susanpieters.com.*

$\mathscr{B}$UDDHA IN A BOTTLE

The genie looked up at me, then looked at the bottle. "You've got to be kidding me," she said.

I wasn't kidding. "You're supposed to fit. Shrink or something."

She pulled up at the corner of her silk pyjama pants. "Laws of physics say you can't make something smaller than it is. Conservation of matter or something. Unless it's a black hole."

"Is it?" I lifted up the glass bottle. It was heavy purple glass, possibly leaded, but surely not heavy enough to be condensed matter.

"What I suggest," the genie said, stroking a finger along my shoulder, "Is that I come live with you."

I remembered the day I'd found the bottle on the edge of the sea, partly covered by kelp, shining in the sun. I'd pulled the cork, thinking there would be wine inside, not a woman. How had she come out of there? There had been smoke. I'd been shocked, dropped the bottle. It had all been so sudden.

She moved her finger to touch my earlobe. "And who knows? Sometime in the future, you may relent and take me up on my offer."

"Three wishes? Never." I'd read all the stories. I knew better. "You've had a week of modern life. Isn't that enough?"

"You can't condemn me to a bottle-life. That's barbaric."

"But it's where you belong," I said, moving away from her soft skin and incense-like perfume. I'd basically been her slave all week, driving her around the tourist hotspots. "Vancouver doesn't have magical creatures unless it's on a film set."

She put her hand out towards the bottle, as if she would grab it and smash it, but she shrank from actual contact. "I can't do it. Please, release me from this curse."

I looked at her tear-stained face. "But that's using a wish."

She got on her knees. "Do it."

"But that's changing the entire ecosystem. That's transferring power — or negating power — that will put the whole universe out of balance."

She prostrated herself. "You have the power to free me."

"What is freedom?" I pulled my feet from her grasp, forcing her to release my made-in-China running shoes. They were a luxury commodity constructed by people who had enslaved themselves to the dream, workers who put up with extreme factory conditions in order to have a better life for their children, while the company executives took the profits to build their own dreams of big houses and offshore tax-haven investments. Even I had bought my shoes for my own personal dreams of being fit, to have knees without pain when I ran, and to look cool. These same shoes I had worn last week when I walked on the beach and found the bottle. "Dreams are funny things," I said. "They're never what you expect. Never really what you wanted."

She could tell I had made my mind up. She got up. She was going to run away, as if running could save her now.

"I wish — " I pronounced loudly, and took a deep breath as she halted her flight, "I double wish, I triple wish — "

She turned to me, fear and perhaps even horror in her face, for she had spent a week with me and knew my habits.

"I forever wish that I never wish for anything more again."

She started laughing then. She laughed until she cried.

I couldn't understand it. "Are you okay? Aren't you going to grant me my request?"

"You solved it!" she sputtered.

"I did? Am I like Spock now?"

"Quite the opposite, you idiot." She laughed. She took the bottle and tossed it in the grey recycling bin that was part of every park's zero-garbage initiative.

"Are you free?" I asked, perplexed.

"More than free," she said. "So are you."

"But I can't wish you free," I said.

"The bottle wasn't my cage," she said. "The wishes were."

"Oh," I said. "Oh."

She embraced me fully and freely. No games, no toying with my ear. "I'd love some sushi right now. Want some?"

"Sure," I said. "That would be—not what I wish for, but …"

"Bonus," she said.

I took her outstretched hand. "Yes. Bonus."

THE SMELL OF ANTISEPTIC

Frances Rowat

Frances Rowat lives in Ontario with her husband, their dog, and a not-quite-startling number of cats. She is most often found behind a keyboard and frequently gets lost in details. Her work has appeared in such venues as Lady Churchill's Rosebud Wristlet, Liminal Stories, and PerVisions. 'The Smell of Antiseptic' was written while her job involved reviewing summaries of experiments that determined the toxicity of various substances. She may be found online at aphotic-ink.com or @aphotic_ink on Twitter.

$\mathcal{T}$HE SMELL OF ANTISEPTIC

Jerem Brand had fled the name Makul and the riches and connections that it might have brought her more than a decade ago, and had settled into the duty schedule of the pioneer physician on Schmid. It was a lonely backwater planet, five years away from any Hub to speak of, and her two rotations there had been mundanely unpleasant.

Schmid seethed with wriggling native life, boasted thirty-hour days, and supported a sneeze of settlers who had dug in to the most temperate of the continents. Brand had heard the last physician had applied for a transfer three times and been rejected twice. The colony was starting to thrive, but there were still accidents, injuries, and individuals poorly adapted to the long and damp days. And every spring, the lindworms came out again.

That morning, the clouds were low and beige, and the spring wind was a chill one. Mackie knocked at the perpetually mildewed doorway of Brand's office. The colony administrator was a slight dark figure carrying a folder. Schmid had computers, but Mackie persisted in handling most of the daily administration on synthetic paper. True modelling computers grew rarer, and time on them more viciously expensive, the further you were from a Hub.

Brand had grown up on an older colony near another Hub, but even there computer models had been rare and precious things. Most of her research studies had, by necessity, involved hands-on experimentation.

"Rieltown needs you out early," Mackie said. Rieltown was perhaps six hours to the west on the shuttle, and Brand was scheduled to visit there in three days. "Lindworm in a kid."

Every year. Brand laced her hands together, rubbing the numb spot at the base of her left thumb.

"How early can I head out?"

"I already had the clinic start triage. See to whoever can't wait, and with luck you can leave by noon." Mackie stepped into the office. "Is there anything you need put on the shuttle?"

Brand shook her head, picked up her computer, and made her way past Mackie into the narrow hall. She took two steps and stopped.

There were rats on Schmid. There were rats on all the Hubs except Scintillation Delta, and so there were rats on nearly all the planets to speak of. Rats dug into grain, carried new and itching parasites and fungi, and were tested in labs. Human and rat alike scratched and hopped their way between planets and across the gulfs between stars. They were a nuisance, but a familiar one.

So it was not the rats themselves which gave Brand pause. Nor how bold they were, watching her openly from down the hall, two crouched and a third reared up on its hind legs.

But these were white rats, all three, while the local ones were brown and grey. Their pale coats stuck up in patches and tufts. She had seen similar mussing on animals with skin lesions, before the scabs and sores drowned their fur.

The one on its hind legs dropped back down and scuttled forward perhaps twenty centimetres. Another sniffed the air, and then all three hissed at her.

Brand was wearing heavy boots, with her pant cuffs tucked in at the top, but she didn't want to try crushing them. It would not be painless and it might not be quick, and the prospect of an injured rat crawling into some part of the camp's infrastructure to die and rot seemed unsanitary at best.

And they were white rats.

"Mackie?" she said, backing away. She glanced into the office, where Mackie was collecting the finished paperwork from its tray. When she looked back, the rats were gone, but she said anyway, "There are rats in the hall, Mackie."

Mackie's mouth thinned. "I'll bring in a terrier," they said. "Have someone check the building and block up any entry points." They picked up the folder and jotted a quick note on it before shuffling the paperwork in. Brand left them to it and made her uneasy way to the clinic.

The only two patients left were a grey-faced old man whose jaw was locked against his pain, and a swollen and anxiously loud off-planet surveyor who insisted on seeing the physician and kept repeating the posted hours.

Brand dealt with them both (a dangerously ulcerated stomach, and an allergy to the pesticides that kept the lindworms away from the spaceport), and then packed her kit and computer and boarded the shuttle Mackie had already programmed. She napped on the way there, as the shuttle hummed its patient way through the chilly skies, and woke when grim brown sleet drummed on the hull.

She woke looking for rats, and didn't sleep the rest of the shuttle trip there.

Rieltown was the closest thing Schmid had to a farming community. It was on stabler ground in the lee of a rocky outcrop, and it grew enough re-engineered wheat to export to the other settlements. It also had the largest herd of goats on the planet. Modern goats made their ancestors look delicate, but the swampy ground of Schmid was not friendly to the animals. They spent much of their time on the outcrop, scuttling around like jumping spiders and eating the tough, twining vines that worked up from the ground, along with any bugs small enough to swallow.

There was quite a lot that was small enough for a goat to swallow. Brand imagined they also ate rats, if they found them.

A goat had wandered down from the outcropping and was skitter-hopping its way down the main street. A small knot of children, old enough to have begun hating the settlement, followed it at a remove of a dozen metres. As Brand left the shuttle and started for the administration building, shivering a little inside her coat and enjoying the expanse of darkening sky after her enclosed trip, the children began throwing rocks. They were small ones, perhaps four centimetres across, and clotted with cold mud. They bounced off the wiry pelt of the goat with a dull plopping sound, and the animal skipped further down the street.

Brand stopped, uncertain of how best to object. One of the children looked at her with flat hate and made ready to throw a rock with her as the target, but another caught their sleeve. "She's the doctor," one of them warned in a thin, high voice. "Yer mam'll be mad."

The first child sniffed and tossed the rock aside. It bounced off one of the buildings with a hollow clatter. Brand watched them for a moment and then walked away, feeling their stares follow her down the street to the Rieltown administration building.

The local manager was a soft-looking woman waiting for her at the building door, and Brand thought she looked guiltier than the situation warranted. Everyone knew not to scratch the site of a lindworm infestation, but in the face of the maddening itch, small children sometimes couldn't manage that much restraint.

"Where did you set up?"

She began walking Brand down the hall. "We've turned the examination room into a sterile environment."

Lindworms had been much more common when the settlers first arrived. Mosquito-like pests, they fluttered on the spring breeze, a loose tangle of wings and burrs. On local hosts, they dug into breaks in the skin, releasing anaesthetic and working their way down into the dermis. They grew to perhaps seven millimetres across, steadily releasing a low-grade anaesthetic as they absorbed nutrients, and sent tendrils up through the skin to shunt waste out of their host.

On humans, the anaesthetic was a mild intoxicant. The tendrils itched and irritated—and when someone scratched at the skin around them, they broke, and the irritated flesh swelled up enough to seal off the shunts. Then the damaged shunt-tendrils died and rotted, and the lindworm, buried deeply enough not to be affected, continued pumping waste directly into the host's system.

If the infestation was treated before the human started scratching, it wasn't a problem; an injection into the lindworm killed it, the waste drained out of the shunts into a bandage, and the next day the foreign matter was removed through a sterile incision. It was intern work.

As long as the human didn't scratch.

It was worse than Brand had feared. The child's left shoulder was a swollen mass, puffy and red, glistening with topical anaesthetic and oozing sullenly. Brand tried for a smile and was rewarded with a low wail.

The manager slipped in front of her and crouched down, managing a smile. "It's all right, Brennan. You're just going to sleep a little, all right?"

Brand excused herself to examine the sterile room. It was hung with boiled sheeting, and a purifier glowed politely, adding a gentle purple undertone to the room's lighting.

She'd worked in worse circumstances. And children bounced back well.

She helped the manager prepare Brennan for surgery, connected leads from her computer to the patient, then scrubbed down and changed in the adjacent room. The manager gloved her hands when she came back in. Brennan lay face down on the table, sterile cloth covering their hair and the healthy parts of their back and antiseptic painting the swollen flesh.

It would have been simpler to cut the healthy tissue out along with the lindworm, leaving the child missing a six-by-five-centimetre cylinder of flesh from their shoulder. But it would take months to get a reconstructive blank to Schmid, and the family probably could not have afforded to ship the organic matter in any case.

The manager began reading off the computer's display in a voice that trembled slightly. Brand wished briefly for Mackie, whose voice never wavered and who always seemed to be neatly out of the way.

Brand did not care for surgeries. The worst one on Schmid had been due to a mauling not long after she arrived. The room had reeked of blood and split bowels, dirt mingling with torn flesh; riding it all, then as now, was the smell of antiseptic.

She had worked in many places over the years. The air in them smelled different, and the brands of antiseptic changed, but there was always that high, biting note.

The scalpel penetrated with a familiar tug and then a sliding give as the flesh parted. Brand bent to examine.

"Doctor?" the manager said.

"Make sure the tweezers are ready." The lindworm's shunts had cracked and swollen from the damage. They were, at least, tougher than the surrounding tissue; if she worked gently, she would not cut them into smaller pieces and leave fragments behind.

Brand sliced a second line into the child's shoulder.

The blood. The shine. The cuts puffing open and spreading in the air. The anaesthetic did its work, and the child's pain went singing down into the void, to wherever lost agony went when it couldn't make itself heard.

Brand ignored the shiver of flesh and began digging out the purplish-brown tendrils of the shunts.

She had always been meticulous in her work.

She set the fragmented tendrils on the tray around the extracted body of the lindworm, assuring herself that she hadn't missed anything. Then she debrided the wound and closed it up. She put in a shunt, which dryly amused her.

"Should be fine," Brand said, applying the final layer of dressing. "They'll probably sleep until morning." She pointed to her computer. "Have someone come and get me if any of the numbers on the display change colour. I'll be in the shuttle."

She left the room, stripping off her gloves and reminding herself that the pain waiting under the anaesthetic was a simple matter of necessity. She'd saved as much flesh as she could; it would press and tug against itself as it knit, but it would be there. The more painful route would leave the child with a fully working shoulder.

It had been the correct decision.

Brand lay down in the shuttle, but she did not sleep. Between the rats from that morning, and the smells of antiseptic and blood, she was awash in memories.

The animals had begun appearing even before she was finished her research: pale staring things, six rats where there should have been four; or a trembling rabbit slunk under shelves in a space almost impossibly small for it, its profiled eye an iridescent dot in the dark. She had thought it fatigue at first, and then sloppiness on the part of the custodians, and then someone's plot to discredit or madden her, someone jealous of her work or disgusted by her testing on animals in the absence of sufficient computer time to run the glittering galaxy of models that were theoretically available.

She had completed her research, but in the end had fled after too many nights disturbed by a frightened gasping in her room or a whine dogging her steps. Her research was well-regarded, and the makulproxen a stunning success.

But the rooms and streets were full of cringing, trembling beasts, and she could not stay.

She bought a new name, and then another, and left. She made it to the glittering Hub and took time, she thought, to heal. The first rat didn't even startle her; she assumed it was a native of the Hub and went on reassuring herself that she had done, ultimately, the right thing.

It had been worth it.

The rabbit scrabbling desperately in the corner of her quarters had shocked her. Confused, she'd picked it up from the corner where it huddled, as she might have a lab escapee. It squealed and wet itself and turned in her hands to bite her, and she let out a short shriek and dropped it. It scuttled in one direction as she ran in another to wash the wound, and by the time the blood was a thin stain on her cuff and she had determined that there was no bite mark, the rabbit was gone.

She turned her quarters upside down twice, methodically, and then hurried away to rent another room for the night.

Her left hand ached from the ball of the thumb all the way up the digit. She could feel where she had been bitten, but there was not even bruising. In time the pain faded, and with it sensation, and the ball of that thumb was ever after numb.

She remembered how the rabbit had twisted like smoke in her hands, and thought of how far she had come. Between the Hub and her home planet was a gulf where nothing travelled except the crashing spectrum of light and radio waves. She imagined the animals struggling to reach her: little minds, little balls of agony, sleeting through the void.

She saw rats in her bathtub, a rabbit in her favourite bar, and when the cat started slinking after her along the concourse, she took herself directly to the travel station and booked passage to another Hub. It cost most of what she had left. She went back to her quarters to collect a few things, heard the skittering inside, and left it all behind without opening the door.

Between the Hubs, travel was faster than light. She thought she could outpace them, and perhaps lose them in the dark.

It had worked, for years.

Brennan was groggy, hungry, and determined not to cry in front of the doctor. Brand examined the shunt and changed the dressing as the manager promised sweets with breakfast and a stuffed animal to be brought in for company.

"There was one with long legs," Brennan said sleepily.

"A teddy?" the manager said.

"Kind of. Like a rat." Brennan began to shrug and then cringed, and Brand bit her tongue. She would have snapped at an older patient to hold still, but children didn't listen.

"There weren't any rats in here, Brennan."

"A big one," Brennan insisted. "With long legs anna furry tail."

"That doesn't sound like a rat," the manager said indulgently, as Brand asked, "Was it white?"

The manager blinked at her. So did Brennan, but with less confusion.

"No, mostly grey. It was …" Brennan waved their right hand in the space between their head and left shoulder. "Cuddling in my sleep. It was growling, but it sounded nice."

Brand felt her mouth tremble and twitched it into a technical smile. "I'm sure it was very nice," she said emptily, and looked at the manager. The manager shook her head and later assured Brand that there had been no such animal. The room they'd set up was not airtight, but nothing larger than a millimetre across could have gotten in, and the purifier would have dealt with anything smaller.

Brand nodded, as if her only concern had been ensuring that the child's wound had not been dirtied.

And she wondered what would come next, now that rats and cats had arrived.

The animals skittered through the colony towns. At first there were stretches of three or four days when she didn't see them, particularly if she didn't need to treat injuries. But like mildew, they appeared more and more frequently as spring on Schmid warmed.

Mackie did not allow Brand's transfer, nor approve her request for vacation.

It ended in late spring.

Brand went to Okafitown, where a man who'd thought he only had a spring cold wasn't getting better. Her patient's face was red and slightly puffy under the sweat that stood out on his skin. She did an examination and sampled his blood, and her computer analyzed the sample and displayed the results to her without comment.

She considered the readout for a moment, then looked up at her patient.

"All right," she said, trying for a reassuring tone and wishing that he was young enough that she could speak to the Okafitown manager instead. "I am seeing some odd results. Your problem is most likely treatable, but I'm going to run a few more tests to find out exactly what you need."

His face didn't turn pale, but his knuckles whitened as he laced his hands together. Brand collected more fluids and smears from him, and fed them into her tools. Most people managed Schmid's thirty-hour days, but occasionally someone's endocrine system grew hypersensitive, rebelled against the odd circadian rhythm, and slipped further out of balance instead of staggering back to a safe range. Then the disruption cascaded through the hectic glands, giddy and cancerous.

The computer blinked its recommendation up at her.

"No," she said.

"What?"

"Nothing," Brand lied. "A message from the administrator popped up over the display. It shouldn't do that. Very annoying." She prodded the screen irritably, pretending to push something aside. The recommended treatment continued to shine calmly up at her.

She had been so proud of her discovery.

"I'll make the arrangements for your treatment with the administrator," she said. "Excuse me."

Outside, the shadows stretched long and sharp-edged and green. Her fingers were clumsy. She tried to scribble a message to Mackie three times before thumbing the voice recording option and resorting to dictation.

Mackie called her back.

Brand nodded a greeting and spoke brusquely. "I've placed the request for his treatment. If you send a confirmation, the Okafitown synthesizer can create it. The manager can begin his treatment, keep an eye on him for the night. I'll leave notes, come back here tomorrow—"

"You should stay overnight."

"That's not necessary."

"The chances of something going wrong are slim." Mackie's tone was agreeable, but Brand did not mistake that for acquiescence. "But if something does go wrong, I'd be glad of your presence."

"I doubt I could do anything the manager couldn't." It was not even a plausible lie.

"You are intimately familiar with the effects of makulproxen, I believe," Mackie said, and Brand's head swam for a moment as the computer seemed to brighten before her eyes.

"I've read up on it."

"I'm sure you did so thoroughly." There was a terrible patience in Mackie's eyes; they knew how badly Brand wanted to leave and would not let her go. She couldn't escape Schmid; she probably couldn't even leave Okafitown without the administrator's consent. "He's important, Brand. Okafitown's surveyor is growing old, and he's the best-trained replacement. I can't chance you not being there."

Brand hesitated.

"Would it matter if he weren't important?" Not to her, surely; she'd want to flee whether her patient were the keystone of the planet's infrastructure or the accidental twin of a planned child. But she needed to know how close she could have come to escaping.

"No," Mackie admitted. "I watch everyone on my planet, Brand. You're here to help them." Their mouth dipped in useless sympathy. "I just try to make sure you're fully committed to helping them."

Brand nodded. The call ended. She stood there for a moment and then went inside, closing the thin door against the dark.

The preparations were not as exacting as they had been for Brennan. She only needed the drug from the synthesizer, and several leads to attach to her computer for monitoring. She swabbed her patient's arm before she attached the medicine drip.

Again, the smell of antiseptic, very faint.

"It's probably best if you try to sleep," she said. "I'll be here in case … It's just a precaution, really."

He nodded. She made a show of occupying herself with her computer, and after a while, his eyes drifted shut.

Brand sat in the young man's room, tracking the drips of light across her screen that showed his breathing, heart rate, cytokine level. The pulsing tumour in his glands shrank angrily, toughening and withering by the moment. His temperature rose as his body grew strong enough to carry away the poisons in his system.

He was sweating out a harsh, high smell of liquorice and gasoline.

Brand could smell it mixing with the antiseptic in the air.

She put her head in her hands.

When the computer beeped to tell her his fever had faded and the makulproxen's byproducts had sunk to trivial levels in his system, she called Mackie.

"He'll be fine now."

"I'm glad to hear it," Mackie said, and Brand was obscurely angry to find that they were not resentful at all of having been awakened. Dishevelled, yes, and bleary-eyed, but that last was clearing up quickly. "Are you coming back now?"

Brand nodded and disconnected. She set her computer down on a shelf in the young man's room; the manager would find it in the morning.

She would have liked to return it to Mackie in person, but she wasn't sure there would be time. If they came to her on the shuttle, perhaps it would carry on; but perhaps the shuttle would be lost with her. She was reluctant to risk one of the settlement's diagnostic machines.

Brand did not turn on the lights as she went. The halls were straight, and the buildings were small, and it was enough to keep one hand lightly on the wall. In the dimness, there was a square of lighter brown against the black; surely the night was past its midpoint by now, and the sky was beginning to come through the darkness before dawn.

She stopped when she heard the soft thump-click of paws in the hall, too loud for a cat and too large for a rabbit.

She guessed what it must be, and, hearing the sounds moving towards her in the darkness, Brand was honest with herself: of all of them, she regretted the dogs the most.

They had trusted her, and had eaten the food she had given them at first. Later, when they were subsisting by gavage and injections, they had cried and snuffled and licked her hands for help as they sickened and died.

Nothing else she had experimented on had hoped so consistently as the dogs.

Brand took a breath and knelt down again, for the last time. The walls were lost in the dark; around her there was only air and darkness and the lonely sounds of pain.

The cat curled at Brennan's shoulder hadn't meant harm. But that was to Brennan, after all. Brand understood it might be different for her.

"I'm sorry," she said. "I wasn't trying to hurt you. I just thought …" She tried to find more words, different or better. She thought of the man sleeping and smelling of liquorice and gasoline in the room behind her. There had been others like him, she knew; in the decade since her discovery, perhaps nearly one for each animal she'd killed. There would be more; there might have been none, had things gone differently; and either way, the animals would always have been hurting. "I thought it was worth it. I'm sorry."

It came closer, a breathy groan at each step. She didn't know if it was angry or lonely. Perhaps loneliness would win out.

Brand held out her hand and waited for its cold touch.

BLOODSTREAM

Nicholas Alti

Originally from rural Southwest Michigan, **Nicholas Alti** *is an MFA candidate at The University of Alabama. He's been a fiction and poetry reader for Third Coast, an assistant poetry editor at New Issues Press, and he is currently an assistant editor for poetry and fiction at* Black Warrior Review. *His work has appeared or is forthcoming in* DIALOGIST, Newfound, Pretty Owl Poetry, Dream Pop, Okay Donkey, *and elsewhere.*

Bl--dstre+m

I've arrived clad in Appaloosa skin and goat hooves
precisely to ride myself furious
until I've outrun me.
What do you think split the seas? A fond hope?
I've swapped mine for this deranged tongue
so when I do ramble off the cliff
I'll not say *dreary this isn't it* but rather
incoherent blathering
a sort of dismal neighing which suggests
I am utterly terrified of anything ambiguous.
I want to know with certainty
how the moon leaks blood
& where the dripping lands.
I'm furious that Constantine saw a vision of the cross
and by this he conquered
though when I hold up the smitten corpse
of some road kill creature in a department store
screaming *BY THIS EXTINGUISHED BODY
I AM VINDICATED*
nobody believes me.

SHOTGUNS AND JINN

Akem

Nigerian-Canadian artist **Akem** *paints backgrounds for the animation industry, writes short stories, and illustrates picture books and comics.* Brown Sugar Babe, *her first picture book, comes out in January 2020. Her portfolio is at akemiart.ca, and you can see her cover art on issues 16, 18, and 23 of* Pulp Literature. *We're delighted to bring her back, this time drawing pictures with words.*

$\mathcal{S}$HOTGUNS AND $\mathcal{J}$INN

Despite the dangers, Mankur didn't mind being a sheriff at an outpost of the Whirling Sands. The Jinn in the desert usually kept to themselves, and it was his job to see that they weren't disturbed by traders, tricksters, slavers, or tourists. In the stifling afternoon heat, he adjusted his cowboy hat, seating it further back on his head so that his crown didn't feel so much like a hot towel wrapped around a headache. His skin was damp, and his wrist-length shirt clung to him like he'd just run a mile in the desert at high noon. Once he started fidgeting, he couldn't stop, and he shifted in his rocking chair and tugged his damp blue jeans away from his crotch. He wriggled his toes and thought about kicking off the too-tight leather cowboy boots crammed on his feet.

Even indoors, the shade from his battered, wooden office was no match for the afternoon sun. If he took off his cowboy hat, the heat would be just about bearable, but removing it would be like admitting that he couldn't handle being a sheriff. Before she'd retired, two years earlier, Sheriff Til had jammed the cowboy hat on his head and clipped, "Good luck." She turned her back and strode out into the desert, never to be seen again.

The five-point star badge glinting on his hat symbolized the promise he'd made to Sheriff Til. And, as the sheriff at the edge of the Whirling Sands, he had to look the part, for himself and any onlookers. He'd be damned if he were to give up and remove the hat because of a little heatstroke and moisture.

With a sweat-stained, off-white handkerchief, he mopped his brow for the millionth time that day then jammed the wet cloth back into his breast pocket. He'd left the door open so he could watch the desert dust devils spin past his view like knee-high tornadoes, flinging dirt gleefully in their wake.

He heard a slight rustle to his left. The prisoner was a strange one — innocent-looking and curled on her side with knees and elbows drawn close. Just after dawn, he'd discovered her trying to steal his horse, and she'd tried to charm him with conversation.

He'd hit her hard with the butt of his gun, and she'd dropped without a sound. Carrying her indoors was sweaty work with the plethora of items he found within a jacket more suitable for winter. When he'd searched her on the hard jail cot, he'd found sharp ornate knives, a ticket stub, a heavy silver candlestick, a hammer, and a wallet in which the ID indicated she wasn't the proper owner.

He found no water bottle, but it was at least a two-day walk from town to this lonely desert outpost. She must have been on the edge of dehydration to sleep so long after a little tap on the head.

There was something about her, though, and he unfocused his gaze, trying to feel magic within her. But the silence suggested that she was city folk trying to make her fortune in the Whirling Sands.

After he'd searched her, he set a cup of water and some plain bread on the stool beside the bed. He gently tugged off the metal rings she wore on every finger. He put the rings and the items from her coat into a small sack and tossed it onto his desk. Later, he would decide what to do with her. It might take days or months to make a decision, but time didn't bother him none. No, he was more concerned with getting back to his routine. By the end of each day, he would feel adrift and insubstantial. But his daily meditation practice calmed his body and focused his mind.

Mankur removed all thought of the prisoner and sank within himself. For a moment, he imagined that there was nothing outside of the endless sand and sky … no desert edge morphing into roads, farmlands, and cities. No people scurrying about on the face of a planet that was over seventy percent water, boasting cities that sprawled across every spot of land. Only this pristine circle of whirling desert existed. He closed his eyes and submerged himself in the vision. He determinedly ignored the trails of sweat trickling over his body like slow-moving snails. Instead, he imagined himself in an oasis of swirling sand that covered the world in silence. He laced his fingers on his stomach and let the quiet move through him, spreading like a balm that soothed the itch and scratch of life that prickled over his body.

A harsh cough ripped through his lungs, breaking the spell of silence. He cleared his throat a few times, his mouth full of the ever-present grit and sand that filled his world. He cleared his throat again, working up a good amount of phlegm, then spat into the bucket beside his desk. The spit glowed for a moment then dimmed. He shook his head, wondering how much magic had strained past his teeth in the two years he'd been sheriff.

Living this close to the Whirling Sands changed folks in ways beyond their control. Sometimes it changed them enough that leaving the desert was hopeless — the magic in the sand became a part of you and held your shape together. Mankur was just grateful that he still had teeth left to chew with, though he could feel the magic chipping like a patient woodpecker at the enamel, carving the once-even rows into jagged shapes. As sheriff, he was authorized to shoot on sight any person who didn't bear the post officer's mark. If spitting out magic-laced phlegm was the price to pay to keep this 'uncivilized' world untouched, he was happy to pay it.

Discovered hundreds of years ago, the raw magic of the Jinn became coveted by the world outside. Back then, a wild gold rush of people flooded into the Whirling Sands, all of them hoping to make their fortunes, despite the blockades set up by several governments. Trails, dirt roads, highways, and railways began to wind their way through the desert. Intricate but desperate transportation systems were hastily built to haul the magical desert sand away. Companies trained thousands of artisans to blow it into specially-designed objects, sealing the magic within.

Suddenly, the Jinn in the sands woke up and took exception to the pillaging of their lands.

Decades of war and high human death tolls forced the world powers to cease access to the Jinn and their magical sands. The Whirling Sands would become a conservation area surrounded by small outposts to protect the desert from disturbance. Many more decades passed, and now only the descendants of the original soldiers remained, greatly changed and forever bound to the sands they could never leave since magic now lived in their bones.

The Jinn postal riders stomped in, trailing dust, their fingers clenched tightly on their shotguns. The two women ignored his presence and, groaning, collapsed on the hard, pew-like benches that lined either side of the door.

Ginny and Lada tossed back their heads and gulped water from canteens, quenching their parched throats. Ginny's dress was covered in mud from the knees down, and Lada's reddened jaw looked like it had been singed by a flame.

Mankur ignored the battered package he'd been about to hand over and picked up his novel, flipping to the page he'd dog-eared.

The package had arrived in the morning, and he'd sent out a call to whoever wanted the job. Ginny and Lada had been working as Jinn postal riders since before Mankur became sheriff. They were born in the desert and so could never leave. But travelling anywhere in the Whirling Sands meant a battle with death, ravenous thirst, and a high level of anxiety from the constant sense of being watched by the wind and sand. He would wait to hand the package over as they seemed uninterested in going back out right away. People moved to their own time and rhythm in the desert and not a moment before.

His mind wandered to the new post officer who had ridden in at dawn to deliver the package. She'd looked haunted, with bags under her eyes and hair standing on end. Her mechanical horse, covered in hair so as not to burn the rider's skin, had exposed patches of metal that were scored and rusted as if burned by acid. Whatever the rider had seen in the desert must have made her anxious to deliver the package and leave before taking a rest. Mankur had refrained from small talk and contented himself with waving goodbye from the door. It was a pity that most city post officers didn't last long enough for him to learn their names.

Before she left, he examined the package, opening it just enough to find a glass globe filled with a fine tan sand, light as snow, twirling in an endless loop. The thick black writing on the cardboard box simply read *Whirling Sands,* with no return address.

Don't ask, don't tell was the policy for packages that returned magic to the sands. It could have been sent by a veteran returning loot, a small government forced to get rid of it, or heirs who decided it was too burdensome to keep.

An hour passed before Ginny's snores broke his concentration. Mankur put down his novel, cleared his throat loudly, and waved the package in the general direction of the two dusty women slumped by the door.

"This just arrived in the mail. Who wants to deliver it?" He didn't yell, so as not to startle them. The sandtrap they lived in was filled with unexpected things that could make a person feel like the shadow of death was just behind them. And with all the weapons attached to their bodies, startling the women could get him shot.

He waited for a response, staring first at Ginny, whose snores didn't falter where she lay stretched out on a bench, one leg propped up on the arm. Her pigtailed, blood-red hair contrasted sharply with her ankle-length, sky-blue dress. When she stirred, hugging her shotgun tight like a stuffed bear, the mud on her dress flaked onto his dusty floorboards. Where she had found mud to trudge through in a desert was anyone's guess — it hadn't rained in months.

His gaze shifted to Lada, awake on the other bench. Her stringy blue hair hung in wet trails over her face. She hunched over her hand-held screen as if she were alone, riding in an open cart on the abandoned railways criss-crossing the desert. Faint laughter came from the device, but nary a smile cracked her face.

Mankur briefly raised his eyes to the roof then shook the package again. The globe rolled and thumped in the box and he set it down carefully and considered other options to get their attention. It wouldn't do for him to break the globe and release the magic within. He was still repairing the facade of his office from the last time something went wrong.

"I'll do it," the prisoner said.

Mankur's eyes tracked left as the prisoner wriggled her stubby fingers through the metal bars, the smile of an angel on her face. He hadn't heard her move, and at Mankur's sideways squint, she shrugged and smiled wider, revealing teeth that flashed like hard diamonds and a dimple that indented one cheek.

"It's just that there seems to be a general lack of interest," she said at his sceptical look. She waved a limp hand around the sheriff's office. "And the other two are already on their missions."

Mankur nodded thoughtfully. She must have been watching the outpost for at least a day to know the other two Jinn postal riders were away on a job. Even locked behind bars, she oozed her easy charm—the same charm she'd used when he'd caught her trying to hotwire his mech horses.

"This horse yours?" she'd asked innocently, patting the rump of the metal piebald horse. The horse's rump gleamed in the hot sun, a patchwork of metal and muscle covered by a blanket and a saddle.

He'd leaned up against the post and rested his hand on his hip, touching the gun clipped to his belt. "Yep," he said, staring frankly at the antique shotgun tied to her back and the rows of metal jewellery that ringed her fingers.

"I thought this was the post office?" With something like regret, she stroked the piebald's mane.

"That's understandable." He'd looked up at the post office sign, which hung by its last few nails. The other half of the sign once boasted a sheriff's star, but Gumdrop had shot it off the day before in a fit of fury, when she'd found out that Grace had taken the last package into the Whirling Sands without her.

"I really should fix that sign." Mankur said out loud. He thumped the package lightly on the table, hoping to wake Ginny, but her snores continued uninterrupted. Lada finally cracked a smile at whatever she was watching on her hand-held and leaned in closer to the device.

With conversation in short supply, he sighed and turned to his prisoner. "So you'd like to take this very valuable package and ride it through howling winds, shifting sands, and dangerous animals to deliver it to the Jinn because of … ?"

She lowered her lashes, and her smile became more modest. "My boundless generosity."

A shine of sweat gleamed on her dark skin, and Mankur empathized, shifting his body and doing his dance with discomfort. Although sweat beaded her face, the prisoner didn't seem to notice the heat—she'd even put on the winter jacket he'd removed during his search. Her hair stood straight up like a mushroom cloud around her head.

Mankur nodded thoughtfully. "And it has nothing to do with the fact that selling the object in the box would make you rich?"

With a slight narrowing, quickly gone, her brown eyes met his gaze. He sensed he'd angered her. Mankur nodded once, his suspicions confirmed. He leaned back in his chair, dropping his gun hand to his hip. He gestured to the post box on the table. "So was this why you let me take you in?"

Her eyes flashed, and Mankur felt himself pinned back by her stare. Her hands dropped from the bars to her side, and her fingers wriggled almost imperceptibly, like a gunslinger about to shoot. Mankur was suddenly glad that, when the piebald's security system electrocuted her, he'd stripped her of those metal rings entwining every finger. Who knew what kind of city weapons tech was woven into those rings?

The security system was a cobbled-together safety measure that he and the Jinn postal riders had cooked up. They were tired of having their horses stolen or disappeared by sandstorms that suddenly grew fingers.

When the silence went longer than he was comfortable with, he asked, just to drown out Ginny's snores, "So what's your name?"

She blinked as if surprised that he would ask, and tightly wrapped her gunslinger hands around the metal bars. To his surprise, she answered, "They call me Kindness."

"Well, Kindness, as you can see, I have my own posse out here that gets paid to deliver goods to the centre of the Whirling Sands." He waved his hand at his uninterested Jinn postal riders. It was a shame that the job attracted those with grit, a high tolerance for danger—and personalities that ignored authority.

He gave himself a firm pat on the head, jamming his hat lower on his crown. He stood and thought, *Time to poke the rattlesnake nest of ladies by the door.*

He didn't relish interrupting Lada's show and Ginny's sleep. But the package had to be delivered soon. Every moment it stayed in the office was a temptation of gold to fortune hunters.

He'd barely taken two steps before he saw a shimmer out of the corner of his eye. He turned around and saw the prison bars dissolve in a shower of sand, like a disappearing mirage.

A low hum reached his ears, and he saw Kindness's closed fists vibrating, squeezed in an empty grip where the round metal bars of her prison once stood.

The bars sifted like sand running through an hourglass, and neat lines of dusty mounds piled up in their place. Then, like a sandstorm, she rushed at him, the edges of her skin trailing dust and a killer grin spreading across her face.

He spun, put his back against the wall, and gripped the gun hanging low at his waist. He raised the package high into the air just as she slammed into him hard enough for the breath to leave his body. On impact, a puff of dust exploded out of her body. He sneezed, then struggled to raise his gun for a hip shot.

She grabbed his gun wrist and firmly jammed the gun deep into its holster, using her grip as a prop to heave herself up and towards the package he held high in the air. Only his height saved the prize, but he became unbalanced when she grasped his wrist and leapt upwards. He listed sideways, stretching his hands in opposite directions as he struggled to free his gun and keep the package away from her.

She jumped a few more times, then hissed with exasperation.

Despite his predicament, he grinned at her, meeting her eyes, which were filled with the glitter of sand and the annoyance of a stepped-on rattlesnake. "I surely am disappointed to have to shoot you for the common thief you are, Kindness. Shame on you, trying to steal Jinn magic for your pleasure."

Mankur hoped that Ginny and Lada had clued in to the tussle. But he could tell from the lack of threats and shooting that the women were lost in their apathy. His eyes shifted back to Kindness, who was examining him with a hard but puzzled frown.

"How long have you been here, Sheriff, for your skin to glitter with magic?" she asked with a building rage. Her eyes flickered with confusion and fear. "How long have I been out *there*?"

Under her gaze, Mankur felt the stuffiness of the room grow thick, and dampness grew in every crevice of his skin. With her grip on his wrist and bicep twisting his body out of shape, his skin was a straitjacket. In a sudden panic, he gathered his strength, ready to heave her off—either with muscle or by the force of magical power within.

Boom!

The wall behind them disappeared in a cloud of dust. Mankur and Kindness dropped low to the wooden floor and cowered. In shock, they looked towards the doorway to see a pint-sized woman standing there, her shotguns smoking and fury in her eyes.

Ginny's snores stopped well after the boom's echo faded, and she jerked herself up into a sitting position. With the back of one hand, she rubbed her eyes and then wrapped her shotgun in the crook of her elbow and kicked out her skirts. She blinked her gritty eyes and looked back and forth from the door to the smoking window, which now let in the biting sun.

"Gumdrop?" It was Lada's soft voice. She'd finally taken off her headphones. "Thought you were off chasing after Grace."

Gumdrop's rage seemed to double her size. Kindness and Mankur flattened themselves on the wooden floor as Gumdrop's fingers twitched on the twin triggers and the barrels glowed red like heated coal.

"Who'd chase after that cow?" Gumdrop said, after a few tense minutes where no one dared move. Her guns had stopped smoking, and the reddened barrels cooled to grey. She dropped the muzzle of her shotguns towards the floor and flopped down beside Ginny on the bench. Gumdrop slumped there like a depressed teenager, except she was pushing fifty and should have retired years ago to a town at the edge of the desert. Or so she kept saying.

"It's about time," said Mankur. But his relief disappeared when a hard hand shoved his head downwards and his lips kissed the floor. When the weight disappeared, he spun around and saw Kindness's legs vanish through the jagged, human-sized hole in the wall made by Gumdrop's shotgun blast.

"Who the hell was that lass?" Ginny asked with a yawn.

Mankur groaned and heaved himself from the prostrate position Kindness had placed him in. He glared over his desk at the three women, all with shotguns in hand, who had let his prisoner escape. "It'd be mighty kind of you three to lend a hand with catching the escapee."

Lada shrugged and looked back down to her hand-held device. "We don't work for the sheriff's office. We work for the JPR."

Mankur picked up his hat from under his desk and fixed it in its proper place, letting it rest lightly on his dome. "Well, then we should help each other—that little lass has just made off with your mail."

Ginny bolted upright and strode out the door with nary a word, rouged lips grim, ankle-length skirt flaring wide, and red hair flaming with the fire of her rage. Lada and Gumdrop looked at each other. Gumdrop shrugged one shoulder and settled into Ginny's vacated spot.

Lada gingerly tapped the red burn on her jaw and sighed. She stood, towering near seven feet tall when she was done rising, though her hunched posture usually brought her down to a mere six. She tucked her hand-held into a plastic pouch and slouched after Ginny into the sunlight, a general air of sullen dampness around her.

Mankur nodded, righted his rocking chair, and straightened out the things that had been knocked from his desk. He carefully set and arranged his ever-present drinking flask, the old paperback book, and a tray full of papers back on the tray. He reached down to adjust his gun, and his fingers closed on empty air.

He spun, mouth agape, and looked at the splintered wall. "Just great. Now she's armed."

"Ain't you going with them?" Gumdrop had settled comfortably into the hard bench by the door. She pressed both hands together as if in prayer and tucked them under one pillow of a cheek, gold eyes staring like a hawk.

"Well, I got no gun." Mankur thought for a minute and strode to the front door and leaned out, checking on the mounts. Only Gumdrop's ride was left tied to the post. "And my horse is gone." With a grudging admiration, he crossed his arms and leaned against the doorway. So that's what she'd been doing when he caught her. She'd pretended she was unable to steal it but had reprogrammed it to meet up with her after she was well rested and ready to flee with the package.

Gumdrop snorted. "Touch Sweetie, and she'll fry you before you get your foot in the stirrup," she said, and fell asleep, snoring loudly between one breath and the next.

While Gumdrop slept, Mankur squinted at the sandstorm wall swirling miles down the road. He imagined Lada and Ginny in that sandstorm, their clothes and hair whipping about, shotguns in hand, in grim determination after a girl called Kindness who stole magic in a post box.

A prickle of warning rushed through him—the trail from the horses led not away from the ever-present sandstorm, but towards it. Generally, thieves try to hightail it away from the danger of the Whirling Sands and the desert Jinn.

"That girl is not quite right," Mankur said out loud, remembering the panic that rushed through him when she caught him in her grip. The magic in her hands was not unusual, but there was something more within her that touched the magic in his skin and threatened to rip it out. He walked towards his chair, ignoring his new window and the harsh, jagged light that hit his desk. He sat with his back to the window, the heat of the desert roasting him like a fire pit.

Deep in thought, he steepled his hands and rocked back and forth. His eyes caught the desk drawer holding Kindness's rings. He opened the drawer; ten rings glittered, one for each of her fingers. He picked up the largest ring, probably worn on her thumb, and examined the craftsmanship.

He saw, on its inside edge, a tiny stamp. Before the world decided to preach tolerance and leave the Jinn and their magic in the desert, artisans created many containment objects. The mark on these rings revealed them to be among the oldest of the lot.

Kindness was a Jinn. He winced as he heard Sheriff Til's voice admonish him. "You have one job, son. Help them home." He'd failed spectacularly in that task, but he had the feeling that Kindness didn't need his help getting home.

Mankur turned to look out at the desert sea framed in his new window and shimmering in the heat of the sun. He'd been tricked thrice over: first his horse hacked before he ever saw her, the next to bring her into the office, and lastly to remove the rings.

He stood and removed his hat to fan his sweating head. In a silent prayer, he wished Ginny and Lada good luck and hoped that their deaths would be kind. He hocked his glittering spit through the window. The spit glowed on the sand, and his message spread outward, gathering speed as it raced across that sea of sand towards the riders. Maybe if the prayer reached them before they reached Kindness, they would turn around.

Kindness rode the sheriff's horse into the sandstorm. Her teeth had rattled when she hit the ground after diving out the makeshift window. She'd run a few steps then given a soft whistle. The horse stepped easily out of the chains she'd loosened and came trotting up alongside her like a loyal dog.

Thankfully, the sheriff kept his horse saddled; otherwise her thighs would have burned from the horse's metal skin. But to Kindness's good fortune, the horse was fully geared and loaded. She now had the horse, a gun, and the post box—three things more than when she'd escaped from the city.

A few minutes later, she heard the soft sound of swirling sand and twisted to see two women on horseback following her. One, sitting side-saddle, was the lady with the long skirt; the other was the stringy-haired woman who had been watching a soap opera that was two months behind the current airing in the city.

Kindness looked down at her horse, who swivelled its ears back and forth, and realized that she hadn't neutralized its locating beacon. The device allowed the horses to stick close together and find each other if lost. But it was too late now to care about being found, and it would be about half an hour before she reached the swirling cloud of sand that was her home and freedom.

She looked down at her strong fingers and wriggled them, marvelling that after ten years of bondage, she was free of the artisan rings that had trapped her in physical form after the war. During the war, the humans had called her War Wind, though she had no name a human would recognize. She was finally free and could slough off the made-up names for what she was. Even the name Kindness was a temporary placeholder that let her pass through the human world without suspicion. But she was Jinn, a whole that encompassed everything, not an individual to be named.

She closed her eyes and tried to erase the names that moulded and hardened her into human form. She'd briefly felt freedom in the sheriff's office when her form softened into sand. But now, under the hot sun and fleeing towards the Whirling Sands, she felt within her the name Kindness—not her city name, or even the name War Wind that was so close to her Jinn form. She panicked, thinking it was all a dream, feeling the weight of those rings once again. But she snapped open her eyes and saw only tan lines encircling her long fingers.

A sharp doubt struck her, as if from the great, blue sky. Could she even return to what she was? Or had she remained a human for too long?

Forced to speak the language of humans, her thoughts and mind had been limited by the words around her. The metal rings reduced her from vastness into a container in the shape of a human skull. Before she'd taken human form, she had not known about time or fear or pain … but she learned.

A shot whizzed past her face, and she ducked down on the horse to make herself a smaller target. Although nothing could kill her now, a bullet could sting and wound the body, and she'd learned to avoid pain. She squeezed her thighs tight around the horse's back, but it was already going as fast as it could, its hooves digging at the sandy terrain.

She turned her mind inward, trying to feel the magic in the grains of sand that seeped into her. She could taste home in the dust that filled her mouth; it stung her eyes and burrowed into her lungs. She felt her body blur, merging with the magic of the sands.

She smiled. Perhaps she wasn't too changed after all. She just needed to immerse herself in the Whirling Sands, and they would rip this body apart for her.

A sudden tightness wrapped around her chest. She looked down as a rough rope cinched hard and yanked her off the horse. She thumped painfully on her back in the sand. Stunned, she lay there, mouth open, gasping for air and staring at the clear, eggshell-blue sky.

"That wasn't so hard," said a bored and impatient voice.

Kindness heard footsteps approach. It felt like they were walking all over her body, so attuned was she to the sand. When she focused her eyes, she saw Lada leaning over her, stringy, damp, blue hair flowing down like a waterfall.

"Did you get turned around, thief? The city is back that way. You're running towards your death," Lada said.

Kindness felt a rising fury that left her throat as she coughed out a cloud of sand. "Thief? What did I steal, you mangy human? You slavers." Rage stuttered her speech and clenched her belly. She turned to her side, the hacking coughs taking over, spraying sand from her throat.

Hooves clopped into view, kicking up sand. She held her weak head up and saw Ginny holding the sheriff's piebald reins—and the stolen post box.

Kindness snarled at Ginny and wriggled her fingers, trying to make a spark, to turn the world upside down, anything to wipe these two from her sight. But she was caught in the middle of her transformation, between human and Jinn. She could do nothing but gasp out sand and glare. The Jinn in the post box was once again held by human hands. Kindness had felt the captive Jinn, tiny but aware, when she first passed by the sheriff's office.

"It's our job to deliver this box back to the Jinn." Ginny had hooked her leg over her pommel and sheathed her shotgun.

"And kill anyone who stands in the way." Lada jerked the rope, and Kindness found herself pulled to a sitting position. She heard a gun cock and felt the coolness of a barrel against her temple.

Kindness bowed her head and closed her eyes, the grit of the sand scraping her lids, and waited bitterly for the shot. Days after escape, and within sight of home, her chosen time of death had been taken from her too.

She waited, but the shot never came. The day grew cooler, as if something had blocked the sun.

"But it never moves." Ginny's voice trembled in shock and fear.

Kindness snapped open her eyes and saw a shadow on the sand. The Whirling Sands had come to her like a silent tornado, as wide as the gaze connecting sand to cloudless sky. Beside her, Ginny and Lada stood, frozen and staring. Kindness, still wrapped in rope, ignored the gun and turned awkwardly on her knees.

Ginny shouted, "Now, we got no beef with you. We just came to deliver this and take this thief away."

Kindness began laughing as the storm, mountains high and curious, hesitated, then moved forward, covering them all with its being. She was still laughing when the sand scoured her clothes and skin, shattered her bones, and ripped apart her human name, scattering her like torn paper, folding her into itself.

She spared no thought for Lada and Ginny. The humans who lived at the edge of the Sands did so at their own risk. Over the years, Jinn magic teased its way into their mouths, seeped into their bones, and glittered on their skin. It changed them into something almost Jinn, like being in the city had changed her into something human. The Whirling Sands were just reclaiming their own.

At nightfall, Mankur finally pounded the last nail into a board of compressed sandwood to patch up the hole in his office. He'd also redone the sign out front to proclaim this building a sheriff's office *and* a post office.

He heard a scraping out front and dropped his hand to his holster before he remembered that he had no gun. He shifted his hat on his head and stepped outside. Three horses huddled by door, their saddles and gear gone. The metal skin on their flanks and neck shone and reflected the remaining light as if they'd just been polished.

He sagged in relief then patted the horses on their heads, tied them up, and activated their alarms. He wondered if Kindness would ever show up again, with her flashing smile and glittering dark skin of sand. If she did, would she be like him? Caught between a Jinn and a human, always both and neither?

Better she didn't return; better she integrated back into the Whirling Sands. With that thought, Mankur tugged his cowboy hat low on his crown and traced its sheriff's star. The star helped him hold his shape well enough. And, unlike Kindness with her rings, he could remove the hat at will—it held no artisanal mark of entrapment.

Someday he'd return to the Whirling Sands, but not today.

Today he would send Ginny and Lada's family the news. Though neither of them spoke much of personal things, it was just good manners to let their next of kin know that they weren't coming back.

He'd been taught that long ago by Sheriff Til.

He walked inside, past Gumdrop, who had taken up residence on the jail's hard cot, and sat in his rocking chair. Even within the office, he could feel the Whirling Sands call him, licking at his skin. He spat magic into the bucket beside the desk and pulled his hat low over his eyes.

When they'd separated from the Jinn to defend their home, the seven of them had been called the Killing Winds and sent to all corners of the earth. The World War on the Jinn had come screeching to a halt soon after. He'd been the Night Wind, and the fourth one to make it home.

He'd wait until all of them did.

THE HUMMINGBIRD FLASH FICTION PRIZE

THE HUMMINGBIRD FLASH FICTION PRIZE

Diminutive but dazzling, hummingbirds charm us with their aerial adventures, fighting rivals and courting mates. Like these bantam birds, flash fiction delights us with dips and dives, zinging across the page. The contenders for this year's Hummingbird Flash Fiction Prize were a strong and agile bunch, challenging rivals and courting admirers. Judge Bob Thurber had this to say about the winner, **Tatjana Mirkov-Popovicki**: "In 'Afterlife', the author skillfully tiptoes around grief and heartache, presenting a nicely woven, quirky portrait of life coming at you, whether you're ready for it or not." And runner-up **Chad V Broughman**'s story 'Featherweight' "was a close contender with an ache all its own."

Thank you to Bob Thurber for his expert judgement and comments, and congratulations to this year's winners. Our avian friends might be headed for warmer climes, but we are ready for winter with these hardy Hummingbirds.

Tatjana Mirkov-Popovicki is an established visual artist and storyteller living in Port Moody, to where she immigrated from Serbia in the nineties. Her literary short stories have been published and earned awards in Canada, the United States, and Ireland. She is presently working on a collection of linked short stories set in Serbia and Canada. To see Tatjana's art and read about her literary journey, please visit her website mirkov-popovicki.com.

*In the flash fiction piece 'Featherweight', **Chad V Broughman** pens the tale of one man's lifelong torment that stems from a single childhood scene. Broughman won the 2016 Scythe Prize and published a chapbook —the forsaken— with Etchings Press. Recently, he was anthologized in* On Loss *and won the First Chapter contest sponsored by Arch Street Press. His fiction is in journals nationwide* —Carrier Pigeon, River Poets Journal, Burningword, Sky Island Journal, *to name a few— and he is nominated for Best of the Net 2019. Chad served as co-editor for the blog Café Aphra and holds an MFA from Spalding University.*

*A*FTERLIFE

BY TATJANA MIRKOV-POPOVICKI

Like a cruel joke, one day after she buried her mother, Air Canada sits Bea next to a bloody undertaker. A manicured index finger taps the gold-rimmed, ornate business card. Mr Robert Lang, Sunrise Funeral Services Inc.

"Just in case," he says in a languorous voice.

"Double whiskey," pleads Bea, snatching the flight attendant by the sleeve. Her neighbour looks alert. He just witnessed her taking two Gravols. Perhaps he saw her earlier at the bar of the Toronto airport grill-lounge, where she drank a few for Mother's soul.

"Tough day?"

There was only one thing Bea and her late mother had in common. They both got a kick from taunting nosy people.

"More like a decade. Where shall I start? A divorce, a daughter in a cult commune on the west coast, and, as of recently, a dead mother. I could have used your services yesterday. The wake catering was ghastly." Bea is painfully aware that Jessica's exotic lifestyle is the only thing separating her from mediocrity.

"I am sorry for your loss. She is with the Lord." Mr Lang isn't too hard on the eyes with his smooth rosy cheeks, save for the straw-like blond comb-over. His gaze scrutinizes Bea's empty glass.

"I doubt it." Bea can't stop herself now. "She's more likely burning her bra in hell. She was a feminist, activist, atheist, maybe even a communist for all I know." She's overdone it. Mr Lang looks like he is about to lay an egg. Poor fellow, stuck for six hours in economy class next to a crazy woman.

"I am sure God will forgive her." He shifts his body toward the window and starts leafing through a sleek, Bible-like black book.

Bea pulls out her phone and searches for the #daughtersofthe-onlyonefaith feed. The top tweet reads, *Your billions should feed the penurious @jeffbezos.*

Jessica wrote that. Bea can recognize her daughter's work by its unique use of words. The cult pursues moguls and celebrities, pleading with them to follow Christ's path. They inspire sacrifice and redemption. *Your opulence is undeserved—repent @parishilton. Save your soul—give up your chattels and real estate @trump.*

She scrolls through the swamp of one-liners, searching for something meaningful: a message meant for her, a sign of love from her child. It's been six years of this, and Bea's shame, guilt, and hope keep churning, evolving, and hurting. Whatever she did to deserve this remains a mystery. Jessica lives in an undisclosed location. She doesn't call or write. Just like Mother's, her attention is solely on saving the world.

Bea shows the feed to Mr Lang. He smiles politely. "She's doing God's work. I hope you find her."

Gravol must be doing its work on Bea since she is almost enjoying the undertaker's company. She hasn't been this close to a man in a very long time. But his pale hands creep her out. She wonders if he dresses up cadavers and puts makeup on waxy, dead faces. Bea almost didn't recognize her own mother laid out in the coffin, an amiable pastel smile gracing her face. She wants to ask Mr Lang if they still embalm the dead and how that's done. She doesn't remember ordering more whiskey, but here it is. It burns pleasantly while the roar of the motors fills her ears. She closes her eyes and imagines the wings of the plane dipped into pitch black, gliding directly to hell.

What happens next is a blur. Bea drinks, talks, has hot flashes, and sweats profusely. She feels very friendly toward Mr Lang, whose first name is Robert. She asks if many of his corpses are middle-aged women, and if he gets to see them naked.

"Your hands are so why-ite," she slurs. "Is that from formal-dee-hyde?"

She stumbles toward the bathroom, splashes water all over her shirt, and for the life of her, can't figure out how to get out. Then there is turbulence, and someone bangs on the door, and two mean, elf-like flight attendants pull her arms and screech because she puts up a fight, you bet she does. Their faces are grinning gargoyles as they push and shove mercilessly until she hears Robert's voice.

"She'll be all right, I promise," he says to the monsters. "Please, give her a break, she had a family tragedy." He gently leads Bea to her seat. Perfectly said, she thinks.

The airplane keeps shaking, and Bea is overcome with dread. Among many other things, she fears that her ex knows where Jessica is. Bea is also afraid of the afterlife. If the plane crashes and they all die tonight, she wishes she could stick with Robert the undertaker. She dreams of falling through the sky. It's gloriously cool, and she is naked, young, and lean like before she had Jessica, when she jogged and hiked and climbed mountains to please her husband before he ran off with someone better. Bea's mother is singing a lullaby in some language Bea doesn't understand. She is a baby in the cradle, and Mother shakes her to wake her up.

Robert's grey eyes twinkle. His comb-over is ruffled, tufts of hair glistening in the pink light of dawn.

"You shouldn't miss the sunrise." His breath smells like clotted cream. Bea's head balloons with ache. She shrinks at the thought of what transpired last night.

"Robert, I am so sorry. Thank you for being so kind to me."

She searches for her iPhone, but Robert's hand finds hers and cradles it ever so gently.

"How about a nice Tim Hortons breakfast after we land?" he asks timidly. "Unless you are in a hurry."

Outside, the sky is an abstraction of red and gold. The universe is blossoming. A tip of a meringue mountain sparkles in mid-air.

"Mount Baker," they say in unison, and they chuckle. Bea is astounded to find herself embarrassingly ravenous.

ℱEATHERWEIGHT

BY CHAD V BROUGHMAN

In fifth grade, I had to write an essay on a topic I felt strongly about. I wrote mine about hunting and called it 'Murderers Amongst Us'. In it, I declared the act of shooting an animal to be homicide, declared hunters to be barbarians. My teacher gave me an 'A' and drew two red stars by my name. For a few days, Ma taped it to the front of the refrigerator but always took it down when she heard Pa pulling in. I asked her why, and she told me there was no use upsetting him.

"Why would it?"

"It's about man things," she said, folding the essay in her hands. "Trust me, I don't understand them either." I must have looked at her funny because she quickly revised her statement. "I mean, all that macho stuff. Kind of silly, don't you think?"

That week, someone's fingers were caught in the belt feeder where Pa worked, and the mill closed early. Ma was in the garden. By the time she heard Pa's truck, it was too late to get to the refrigerator. It was quiet at the dinner table except for intermittent food talk like "Pass the mashed potatoes" or "More corn?" And the bare space where my essay had been was awkward and blaring, may as well have been a naked stranger standing there. The next day was Saturday, and Pa left without a word. A few hours later, he returned, sloppy drunk. He stepped from the truck and ambled to the porch where Ma and I stood. In one hand was my essay, rolled into a cylinder; in the other, dangling from his index finger, was a new pair of boxing gloves.

They were Everlast brand, light brown and vinyl. "Already shaped, don't gotta make a fist," he said, turning them back and forth like a game show host. "Just slide your fingers in, and they curl up on their own." When he pushed the gloves toward me, Ma stepped to my side, pulled me close, and stroked my hair, hard. She told me to thank him for the thoughtful gift. But my tongue wouldn't move. Now I understood what she was trying not to say just days before. Pa thought me a milksop.

"Take 'em boy, they ain't gonna bite." I held out my hands, and Pa put them on me — the foam padding soft, rubbery — and drew the strings tight. Though the gloves felt clumsy, like winter boots strapped to my hands, in that moment, I was the reason for the atta-boy gleam in his eye. Then Pa returned to the truck, stuck his upper body through the open passenger window, and reappeared with another pair of gloves, bigger ones.

My heart flopped. My face flushed red, hot.

Pa stepped near but said nothing, just tapped his padded hands together and nodded toward the yard. I looked to Ma, but she turned away. I plodded after him onto the front lawn. Then he stopped, spun around, and started ducking and diving, drunkenness making him sway some. Though Pa's sparring was gangly, I was terrified.

"Dukes up, boy," he said, dancing half circles around me. I stood like a statue. "Guard yourself," he shouted, jabbing just past my ear with his right, crossing with his left. I raised the gloves in front of my face, palms in, but my legs wouldn't move. The louder he yelled, the more immobile I became.

"Put 'em up, damn it!"

"I can't. I just—"

Pa stopped hopping and slowly lowered his arms until they hung at his sides. An eternity passed while he stared at me. I tried to maintain his gaze as best I could. His eyebrows pulled down and together. His lips narrowed, nostrils flared. Quick as a copperhead strike, he threw a right hook. We were like two pistons: his glove smashed into mine, then my own fist struck the bridge of my nose. My neck snapped, and I stumbled backward. I remember the sound of his laughter, big and devilish. It felt like the whole world was watching. Though the sting from the blow didn't come right away, my cheeks were burning. I wanted to run away, but that seemed even more humiliating. After regaining balance, I pulled myself upright to face him, and a nervous chuckle slipped out, more like a high-pitched cheep to my own ears.

Pa was silent again, his eyes wet and glassy. My breaths were short, like I'd swallowed a cork and it stuck. I tried to tug at the collar of my shirt, but with my gloved hands, I couldn't grip it. Then I crossed my arms, uncrossed them, and crossed them again. At that point, the bite from Pa's punch set in. The skin on my face tightened, and my nose had a pulse. When my lower lip began to tremble and the tears welled up, I pleaded with myself, *stop squirming*. But the tears spilled out anyway. I cast down my eyes and thought, *Oh God, I am a sissy*.

Though I didn't look up, I could hear Pa ripping off his gloves, the vinyl scrunching and creaking. They thudded at my feet when he threw them down and traipsed past me with a wobbly gait. I glimpsed over my shoulder in time to see him ascend the porch stairs. The sun had risen, and its rich, yellow rays were full across his back. I thought he looked like a god, a fearful one. Without turning around, he said woodenly, "Put the gloves away." Then the screen door banged against the door frame.

I knew then that one day I'd recover from Pa's disappointment in me, but when I looked to the kitchen window just in time to see Ma duck out of sight, I was down for the count. It would take a lifetime to pull myself up off the mat, to figure out which of the three of us shamed her most.

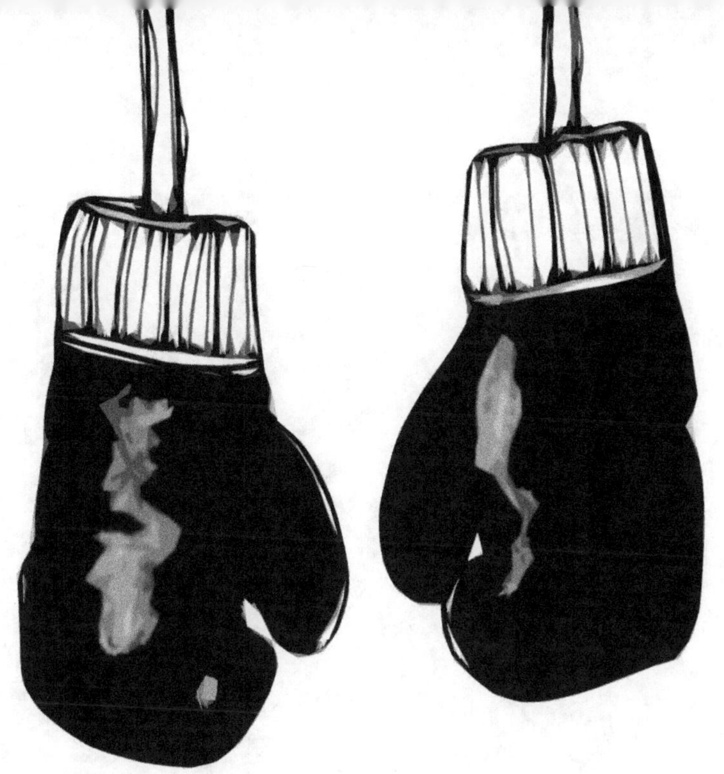

Four awards for genre-busting fiction and poetry

The Bumblebee Flash Fiction Contest

Deadline: 15 February

Prize: $300

The Magpie Award for Poetry

Deadline: 15 April

First Prize: $500

The Hummingbird Flash Fiction Prize

Deadline: 15 June

Prize: $300

The Raven Short Story Contest

Deadline: 15 October

Prize: $300

For more information visit: pulpliterature.com/contests

Short stories, poetry, and comics you can't put down.

GHOST ROOM

Allison Bannister

Allison Bannister is a cartoonist and comics scholar based in New York's capital region. Her work often utilizes fairy-tale themes with modern twists and has been published in numerous small press collections, including the comics anthologies Wayward Sisters, Local Haunts, and My Kingdom for a Panel. You can find more of her work at basictelepathy.com.

South Eastern
University
Exit 6

Exit
6

Fuck
this.

Recalculating.

Beep
Beep
click

Years Ago
Freshman Week :)

1:37 PM Sat June 16
Beep
click

Leigh!
Leigh.

Leigh, are you coming?
Julie?
Matt and Sara just got out of class. Are you coming to lunch with us?
What are you doing here?
Um, it's Tuesday?

Right, I just--
I thought you had something going on?
More important than lunch with you guys?
Never.
Ha, right. I guess not.
Argh.
My Shakespeare class is going to make me crazy.

Too much Iambic Pentameter?
We're reading The Taming of the Shrew.
I remember it being bad, but oh my god it's so much worse.
I just want to shake some sense into Kat,
and get her out of that god-awful relationship.
It's that bad?
I don't even know where to begin,
But... I kinda love some of the sonnets.
Shall I compare thee to a summer's day?
Naw, there's this whole string of poems that are pretty obviously about some guy Shakespeare has a major crush on, and given our culture's idealization of Romeo and Juliet and young hetero love I just think it's fabulous that Shakespeare was probably queer.

That doesn't really surprise me?

I always liked how easily Shakespeare's characters swapped genders, how thin those lines were. It's kinda comforting to see something so influential that almost has space for me in it.

I know, right?

There's all kinds of room in Shakespeare's plays for gender fluidity and ambiguity

but the guy must have been super repressed. The way the plays all end...

everyone dead or married...

Shall I never see a bachelor of three-score again?

Oh, Much Ado is so problematic!

But I still love Beatrice and Benedick.

If banter be the food of love, I'm sure I'll never be lonely.

I miss you.

What do you mean, miss me? I'm right here.

It's stupid because Amber is great and you seem so happy, but this is how I loved you best.

I don't know anyone named Amber.

Not yet, but...

I hated all your girlfriends.

I wanted so badly to tell you I was in love with you, but I was scared I would lose my best friend.
But we lose this anyway.
We move apart and have our own lives and then you call me up out of nowhere, asking if I'll be a bridesperson.
and there's this ugly yellow dress
and beautiful pictures of you and Amber all over facebook.
and I tell you that I would love to do it, that I'm so happy, but I'm not--
I feel like there's a spear in my chest
and the world is out of oxygen
and it's too late to go back
to tell you how I feel.
I love you too.
You...
What?

I love you and I want to be with you.
but you--
It can be just you and me forever.
Julie--
We'll date through the rest of college.
break up to pursue our dreams
then reunite
because love conquers all.
We'll be married in June.
The wedding party will wear rainbows.
We'll never be lonely again.
We never--
We never what?
You always loved me.
How do you know I never loved you?

Don't answer that.
It might be important.
More important than this?
More important than us?
Julie...
Whatever this is, it's not real.
This isn't you. There never was an "us".
And you love Amber like crazy.
Julie calling
Hello?

Where the fuck are you?!
L.
I stopped by South East U.
I'm close.
You're late.
The photographer is already bugging me about pictures with the bridal party.
You had better be here and be dressed before I cave and start without you.
I'll be there in a few minutes.
You better be!
Hey, Julie?
Yeah?
Why yellow?
I dunno.
I wanted rainbows.

TREASON'S FULCRUM

JM Landels

$\mathcal{T}$REASON'S FULCRUM

Lauraign leans close to me, her eyes sparkling with mischief. "Think, Irdaign. It will be so easy. And more ... so fun."

When she laughs, my twin sister reminds me of a fox, her grass-green eyes and white teeth glinting in the sunshine.

"We don't look enough alike. My eyes are blue—"

She waves an impatient hand. "And my hair's straighter. Details! Compared to most Ilmari, we're as like as two eggs in a nest. Look!"

She takes a lock of my hair, holds it up between our faces, and starts to sing. As she does, the tight ringlets I've fought all my life to tame relax and soften, flowing over her hand like water. Intrigued by the possibilities, I add my voice to hers, a counterpoint melody that deepens the colour, turning it from pale strawberry blonde to a rich, bronzy red that matches hers.

She sits back, hands on hips, mock put out. "See, you're better at it than I. You've been teasing me all along."

I fold my arms. "We're good, Lauraign, but not that good." I flick my mismatched lock over my shoulder. "Can you change the shape of your face, the colour of your eyes, and the timbre of your voice all at the same time? And maintain it?"

She laughs. "I don't even need a charm to do your voice, Irdaign," she replies, in, I'm annoyed to admit, a quite passable impression of me. "I've been practising for years."

The tip my sister has received from her friends, such as they are, is this: Prince Goffree of Brandishear, as part of his war with the Valnirati, has drawn up land grants—hundreds of them, prepared in advance—to be awarded along with concomitant titles to his captains and generals. Such deeds, worthless as they are now with the territory under Ilvani control, will be worth a fortune should the war end in Brandishear's favour.

Not that my sister and I want to rob the worthy soldiers of their rightful pay. But two or three deeds fewer will not affect the officers. There will be more deeds than heroes by the end of this bloodbath, and excess lands will go to already-titled lords, who have no need of further riches as far as we are concerned.

What does concern us is the parcelling up and selling off of land. We Leisanmira have found our travels more and more restricted with each passing year. In peacetime we wandered freely between Ilmari and Ilvani lands, hindered by none, welcomed by most. But now suspicions run high, and trust is hard to come by. More and more often we have to drive our carthorses around manors that once let us pass through with ease. If the borders of the Valnirata are eaten away by more Ilmari landholders, our routes will become ever more circuitous. A few well-chosen landlords, sympathetic to our people, could keep our trails open.

It is our good fortune Prince Goffree has chosen as his clerk for this task not one of the household scribes inside the Bastion but Hrinmeath Udor, a lawyer situated in Harkness square.

It takes a fortnight of careful scrying and old-fashioned spying to track the habits of both Udor and his son, Molod; it takes a week more to introduce myself—or rather Lauraign and me, both of us playing me—to Molod. There follow several evenings of flirting, teasing, softening, yet ever refusing to follow him home from the Three Rings in Glaeddyn Lane. Tonight his luck will land.

Molod lifts the flagon to pour me more wine. I put a hand over my cup, lower my eyes, and murmur something about him taking advantage of my weakness for drink. He would lead me home now, but I demur. I am too modest to be seen walking arm-in-arm with a young man of the town into his home. I ask instead for a token I can show to his footman, so I can arrive after dusk. He is about to pull the signet ring from his finger but pauses, no doubt thinking I will simply scamper away with it. Instead he gives me a password.

"Udreyathrin." I repeat the word—his grandmother's surname—enunciating clearly for the benefit of my sister, whose scryed reflection nods at me from the dregs of my wine cup. "I will come after twilight," I say, letting my fingers trail along his cheek. "Wait for me."

I step from the tavern and walk a few feet from the door, singing a charm to transform my blue cloak to brown and weave a glamour of obscurity around me. He emerges shortly after, and I fall into step twenty paces behind him, mingling with the early evening crowd on Rheran's streets.

The most difficult part of this confidence trick is coming now. I strengthen my charm and move it down below the level of vocalization, maintaining an aura of near invisibility as I close the distance between us. It is not long before his father's townhouse appears. Luckily the front door is in shadow, which means the setting sun can cast none of mine. I let my cloak slide off my shoulders, and it fades back to blue near the cellar entrance.

I am on Molod's heels, barely daring to breathe, my footfalls parroting his as he opens the front door and enters.

The gloom of the hallway hides me more, and I stand in the shadows, silent, breath still held, while he flings his coat on a tall-backed chair and calls for the footman. He delivers the instructions to let me in when I arrive and orders food to be sent to his chambers. Molod heads up the marble staircase, and the footman retreats to the kitchen, leaving me alone and gasping for breath, my head spinning in the wake of the effort it's cost me to remain unnoticed.

I poke my head into the drawing room and, finding it deserted, allow my body to follow. The footfalls overhead subside, and there is the sound of a door closing. I assume Molod is in his chambers, which must be directly overhead.

I don't have long to wait before dusk falls and the large brass door knocker sounds. I watch from the drawing room as the footman opens it to my sister, her hair showing curly and pale where it rests on the shoulders of my blue cloak.

The footman leaves to announce her, and while she waits at the bottom of the stair, I reveal myself to her. I twist our mother's silver dragon ring from my index finger and pass it to her. My hand feels cold and naked without it, but she will need it, both for the continuity of our disguise and for the music-enhancing charm wrought within it.

As the eldest twin by a matter of twelve minutes, I inherited our mother's effects, and Lauraign inherited our father's, when the pair of them became casualties of the early Valnirata incursions.

By coincidence, I inherited most of mother's spellsinging abilities as well. In that sense, Lauraign needs the ring more than I, but it is hard to part with even temporarily.

Footsteps at the top of the stair herald Molod's appearance, and I sink back into the shadows, reinforcing the charm that lets his notice slide off me.

"Naressa." He bows, sweeping his house-robe out in a flourish. "I had begun to doubt you would come."

"Tchah, my lord," Lauraign replies. "I'm not even fashionably late." I cannot see her face from where I stand, but I know the reproach on her lips is accompanied by a scolding and irresistible smile. "Will you not escort me to your table?"

He blushes and stumbles slightly as his gallant poise is overturned by her superior charm. She is so much better at this than I am.

I follow up the stairs, careful not to let my additional footsteps be heard. Molod and Lauraign turn to the right, where a short corridor ends in the door to Molod's apartment. To the left, then, must be his father's chambers.

We have no idea if Hrinmeath Udor is in. I try the door handle, curving an aura of silence around it. It is locked, and the keyhole is blocked. Either it has a falling cover, or the key is in it on the other side. I lean close, as if whispering in an ear, and sing yet another tune, feeling with my voice the weight and resonance of the tumblers. It is a simple enough spell, one almost every gipsy child with any hint of talent learns by accident: how to make things lighter by singing their resonance up the scale. But I am rather proud to have thought of this application for it.

With the tumblers deprived of their mass, it is simple to reach a hairpin into the lock and release it. Weightless or no, the tumblers still make an audible click when they move out of place, and I re-establish my shield of silence, waiting five long breaths before moving again. I have my hand on the doorknob to try it again, when the footman appears at the top of the stairs, a tray of comestibles in hand. I freeze, heart pounding, hoping the spell is still strong.

In the gloom it seems it is, for the footman's unnoticing gaze slips over me without so much as a stutter. It is several neverending minutes of still silence before he leaves Molod's side of the house and descends the stair.

At last I turn the door handle, letting it open a crack. No sound or movement from within indicates anyone is there to notice me, but I am not so incautious as to open the door fully yet. I wrap the blurring charm around me, expanding it to penetrate the door from floor to ceiling, and slowly, with motions that seem slower than the melting of snow, ease myself and my illusion into the room.

It isn't empty after all. The senior Udor is seated at a banking desk, his bent back toward me, nothing but the top of his bald head with its fringe of white hair showing above his thick velvet robe. I close the door behind me and stand in the corner, still as a heron, blending in with the shelves of books and ledgers, letting the illusion settle around me while I ready yet another song.

This one is a lullaby, and it is the hardest one of all, for I must sing it without it being noticed. I begin it softly behind my screen of blurred sight and sound, waiting for it to grow and permeate the room on its own. Gradually, I let my first charm die out, so the nursery charm overtakes and replaces the silence imperceptibly, blending in with the scritching from Udor's pen and the soughing of the wind in the trees outside. I want to make him sleepy, to convince him to retire to the bedchamber, but not to knock him out in his chair.

He yawns, stretches, scratches his head, and goes back to work.

Patience, I tell myself, though my throat is becoming dry, my breath more ragged. I must not falter now. Lauraign should be even now singing the very same song to Molod.

Another yawn. More scribbling. His hand slows, trails off the ledger, and his head jerks him back awake.

Too much. He is drooping in his chair.

I lighten the tune, add words that echo the coolness of fresh sheets, the softness of down pillows, the warm dark of a curtained bed.

He yawns and stretches again, and this time he stands up, never noticing the song now filling the room.

I am frozen but for the parts of my breath and lips that need to keep the song going. Any movement, and my camouflage will dissolve.

He shuffles away to the bedchamber, closing the door after him.

Part of me wants to dash to the desk right away and search for a key to the safebox I know lies beneath the heavy wood. But caution keeps me singing till I feel my throat must surely constrict and choke me of air.

I move to the bedchamber door and sing so my voice resonates through the wood.

It is a risk to check, but I must know. I open the door, and I am rewarded by the sight of Hrinmeath Udor stretched flat out on his bed, one foot dangling, his prow-like nose pointed to the ceiling and reverberating with snores. Out of kindness, or perhaps prudence, I move to the bed and lift that one leg onto it. He rolls over, his snoring softening, but he doesn't awake.

Satisfied, I leave his bedchamber door closed behind me and begin a search of his study for the key to the safebox. I have turned up nothing when Lauraign enters, causing me to drop a bottle of ink. It falls with a loud crack on the wood parquet and rolls across the room, unbroken. Lauraign scoops it up. She returns it to the desk, a smile on her face. It is like staring at a mirror, except the countenance across from mine is radiant, the thrill of danger making her eyes sparkle and the blood rise in her cheeks.

I, on the other hand, am trembling with both exhaustion and nerves. It is not just our talents — hers for deception and sleight of hand, mine for the Leisanmira magic that is our birthright — that differ. She thrives on intrigue, risk, and the thrill of proving her wits; and while I can play such games, they take a heavy toll on both my physical and moral being.

"I haven't found the key," I whisper, my voice cracked with fatigue.

Her eyes glisten in the light of the moon, rising through the mullioned window. "No matter." She pushes her sleeves past her elbows, clenches and unclenches her fingers: the master burglar setting about her work.

"It may have wards," I remind her. And in fact it does glow faintly with the lines and traceries of magical seals.

"Leave it to me, sister," she breathes. I can taste her anticipation. "This magic, I am good at."

I nod agreement and fade back to the study door, cracking it and peering out in case the footman returns.

"And Molod is asleep?"

"Like a babe in the cradle," she replies, not moving her focus from the work in front of her.

I am apprenticed to our midwife, and I know a babe seldom sleeps soundly in a cradle, but I do not argue the point. Molod would have been easy to sing to sleep after the tincture I dropped into his drink and the underlying suggestions I left on his subconscious earlier this evening. Even Lauraign, with her less potent voice, should have had no trouble there.

Still, it couldn't hurt to check, and reinforce the spellsong if I can eke out a few notes.

I leave Lauraign to her work, tiptoeing out the one door and crossing the thickly carpeted landing to Molod's. I ease the door open and put my nose in to assure myself the son still sleeps.

He doesn't.

He is sitting on the bed, a glass of brandy in one hand, a loaded crossbow in the other.

"I wouldn't move too suddenly," he says in a low, calm voice. "I've had a lot to drink tonight, and this has a light trigger."

My heart is thudding triple time as I raise my hands slowly to show I am unarmed. The door has swung wide. At his nod I come through and kick it shut with my heel. There is one small relief in this lake of trouble I've landed in: at least Lauraign can continue undisturbed, for now.

He motions with his glass toward the bed, sloshing brandy. "Sit."

I try the innocent tack, eyes wide, wishing I had my sister's acting skills. "Molod," I whisper. "My lord. You … you fell asleep, and I stepped out to relieve—"

He waves the crossbow, and I stop mid-sentence, having no doubt he is telling the truth about its trigger.

"There's a closet right there," he says, pointing with his brandy at the garderobe behind him, his words not nearly as slurred by drink and enchantment as they should be. "What you meant to say is relieve us of some of our valuables."

I say nothing, refusing even to blink.

"Pity for you my apartment's sewn up with warding spells. Against poison, malice, and gipsy charms." His look of smug vitriol chills my blood.

I think of my sister back in his father's chambers, unaware of any such warding. But no, Hrinmeath Udor's sleep was sound—I felt it in my bones when the music entered him. His rooms must have no such warding, or else I would have sensed the same oppressive muffling that now fills my ears and throat like a head cold.

Molod leans forward, resting the crossbow on his knees, its bolt still pointed at my heart. "I'm surprised you came back, though. Or was it that you couldn't find this?"

He stands up, the bow wavering unnervingly, and sets the brandy down. From behind his back he draws an Ilvani bloodblade.

I can't stop the involuntary intake of air, but he seems to take it as frustration rather than surprise. All at once this game has gone from mildly dangerous and potentially profitable to something much darker.

Lauraign, I know—I hope—will have retrieved the deeds from Udor's safebox by now. She is nothing if not an expert lock-breaker.

I strain my ears, listening for movement, wondering how long she will need to leave safely, hoping she will not wait for me. It takes all my self-control not to yell out a warning and at least let her flee to safety. But Molod's finger is still on the bow's trigger.

I try to settle on which lie to use. Will he even believe me if I tell him truly I'd no idea there was a bloodblade in his possession?

And will it even matter? Now I know of it, my life is a liability to him. Unless ...

I take a breath, relax my mind's eye, and call the Sight. It is an unreliable gift at best, not nearly so well-developed as it will be when — if — I grow older. Asking for it is like asking snow to fall from a clear blue sky.

And yet weather, capricious as it is, sometimes cooperates.

Images flash through my mind. I shut them out. I don't need pictures, I need sounds. Names.

"C-caradar ..." I stutter out, throwing the dice and wondering whether this name will save or sentence me.

He stiffens.

Still groping for which turn to take, I commit further. "... is uncertain."

The worry on his face ushers in more images. I let them come this time, flooding my mind's eye, and I see it: the dagger passing from hand to hand in a secret pact.

"He does not trust the Boar." I let the words come, throwing them together in a last-minute soup without knowing what they mean. "Doesn't feel the arrangements are secure ... or secret enough." I nod to the knife, bluffing furiously. "It seems he is right."

Molod has blanched, lowered the crossbow, and is leaning against the sideboard. My muscles tense, watching for my moment.

And then I'm hit with another vision, this one unasked for. This knife has been forged to take the life of Goffree of Brandishear. All — though it is a large 'all' — I need do is kill this man, take that dagger, and save the life of a prince.

But the visions won't stop. Colliding possibilities ricochet in my head, sending waves of nausea that double me over, retching.

There is a clatter as he drops the bow, its bolt shooting across the floor beneath the bed.

Despite the nausea I launch myself forward, knocking the knife from his hand. I pick it up, prepared to run, then drop it as if it burns me. Too late, for a maelstrom of visions have bled from its cursed handle into me.

Goffree lives, the war drags on, and life after life is squandered. Goffree dies, and with him all his heirs, leaving the Black Boar of Holden on the throne; the treaty fails, and Ilmari fight Ilmari while Ilvani wait quietly for the dust to settle. Goffree lives, and the Ilmar is left fat and soft, too weak and helpless when the dragons come. Goffree dies, and from three generations of bitter ashes, a hero rises to unite Ilmari and Ilvani at last.

All I need do is remove this dagger from play to save the life of the Prince. All I need do is leave it here to end his life and sow a peace that will not flourish for far too many decades in the future. And now this choice hinges on me, not because I am wise enough to choose, but because I have the misfortune to be able to See. One path leads to far-off and potential chaos; the other is treason. Both have death strewn on either side.

Unless … unless …

The Sight is reeling past me still, waving fluttering threads of possibility. A strand pulled here, another passed over, yet another turned back on itself. There is a path through the tangle, if only I have the skill to navigate it.

Sick with guilt, crushed by the weight of foresight, I let the dagger lie, and flee the house in my sister's wake.

When the prince I marry ascends to the throne and I lose my daughter to the state, I will remember: this is the price of treason. When I hold my newborn granddaughter in my arms, I will rejoice, and hope the narrow path she treads will absolve me.

§

For more of Irdaign's story, pick up Allaigna's Song: Overture *and the soon-to-be-released* Allaigna's Song: Aria *from pulpliterature.com or wherever good books are sold.*

Allaigna's Song
Aria
JM Landels

Allaigna's Song
Overture
AMAZON #1 BESTSELLER
JM Landels

THE ARTISTS

Ann-Marie Brown

Cover artist, On Thin Ice — Red

Ann-Marie Brown is a Canadian painter working in encaustic and oil. Right now she's painting out of a studio on the west coast, in the company of bears and rain.

The cover piece — *On Thin Ice* — is part of a body of work completed during a six-month residency at the Artsu studios in Helsinki. The early years of Finnish independence were defined by a flight to the edges of ideology, a pattern the artist sees repeating itself in North America. In researching the conflict that ensued, she was interested in what was built from the ashes and curious about what can be learned from the hard-won lessons of that place.

Allison Bannister

Artist, 'Ghost Room'

Allison Bannister lived in three different states during the years she spent writing and illustrating 'Ghost Room'. She currently lives in New York's capital region with her partner Tom and cat Elspeth, where she is pursuing a PhD in communication and rhetoric with a focus on comics composition. Her work often summons up fairy-tale themes in new contexts and follows characters searching for a way home. She has been published in numerous comics collections, including TO Comix Press's award-winning anthology *Wayward Sisters* and the comics-in-a-box collection *Dog City #3*, and she was an editor for the quirky superhero comics anthology *Who is the Silhouette?* Her comics have also been featured in several gallery shows, including a solo interactive art show titled *Food Comics*. You can find her work online at basictelepathy.com.

Mel Anastasiou
In-house illustrator

Mel Anastasiou loves drawing for *Pulp Literature* because she loves the stories she illustrates. She draws in black and white, working from imagination and inspired by details from Renaissance compositions. You can find more illustrations, as well as writing tips and news about her books and novellas, at melanastasiou.wordpress.com, and see her artwork on Facebook at Bird and Branch Artwork.

HALL OF FAME

These are the heroes — the Patrons and Pulp Literati whose monthly support helped bring you this issue. Please lift your glasses and give them a rousing cheer!

The Landlords
Adam Fout
A Bursewicz
Rapscallion

The Innkeepers
Ada Maria Soto
Dana Tye Rally
Margot Landels
Ev Bishop
Shannon Saunders
Roger & Anne Anastasiou
Kevin Harris
Richard Ohnemus
Robin McGillveray
Sarah Farr
Gillian Gardiner

The Cicerones
Susan Lefeaux

The Bartenders
Alana Krider
Richard Gropp
Ron Graves
Kristen Mah

Michelle Balfour
Robert Bose
Victoria McAuley
Dave Wayne
Scott F Gray
Abigail Bruce
Patrick Bollivar
Dietra Malik
Elaine McDivitt
Joshua Pantalleresco
Emily Lonie
Anna Belkine
Shannon Sinn
Katriona Greenmoor
Famille Bussières
RS Morgan
AD Bane
MultiverseJumper
KT Wagner
Michael Weckworth
Danny Palacios
Terry Fries
Sarah Pendergraft
Deepthi Atukorala
Margot Spronk

The Regulars
CC Humphreys
Marta Salek
Rina Piccolo
Jenny Blackford
Jain Cairns
Michael Barrie
Tom Jolly
Leo X Robertson
Kristene Perron
Akemi Art
Peter Halasz
Jennifer Timer
Kristan Cannon
BC
JW Horton
Walter
Miriam Zibkoff
Meredith Frazier
Heather Ane Wilkey

The Clientele
Kathy Denton
Ray Hsu
Melissa Hudson

If you would like to join the ranks of these worthies you can become a patron on Patreon at patreon.com/pulplit, or join the Pulp Literati through our website at pulpliterature.com/join-pulp-literati/.

MARKETPLACE

Books

Advent *by Michael Kamakana* · We thought we knew what the aliens wanted. Think again. · pulpliterature.com/advent

Allaigna's Song: Aria *by JM Landels* · The long-awaited sequel to the best-selling Allaigna's Song: Overture. · pulpliterature.com/allaignas-song

The Labours of Mrs Stella Ryman: Further Fairmount Mysteries *by Mel Anastasiou* · Trapped in a down-at-the-heels care home. You'd be cranky too. · pulpliterature.com/stella-ryman-and-the-fairmount-manor-mysteries

Paperboy: A Dysfunctional Novel *by Bob Thurber* · Photography by Vincent Louis Carrella · shantiarts.co/uploads/files/thurber_paperboy.html

What the Wind Brings *by Matthew Hughes* · Epic slipstream historical fiction · pulpliterature.com/product-category/novels/matthew-hughes

The Writer's Boon Companion *by Mel Anastasiou* · Thirty Days Towards an Extraordinary Volume · pulpliterature.com/subscribe/the-bookstore

Bookstores

Book Warehouse · 632 Broadway W, Vancouver, BC V5Z 1G1 · 604-872-5711 bookwarehouse.ca

Myth Hawker Travelling Bookstore · Canadian authors · Canadian content · small and independent press · mythhawker.ca

Phoenix On Bowen · 992 Dorman Rd, Bowen Island, BC V0N 1G0 · 604-947-2793

Village Books & Coffee House · 130-12031 First Ave, Richmond, BC V7E 3M1 · 604-272-6601 · villagebooks@shaw.ca

White Dwarf / Dead Write Books · 3715 10th Ave W, Vancouver, BC V6R 2G5 · 604-228-8223 · whitedwarf@deadwrite.com

Western Sky Books · 2132-2850 Shaughnessy St, Port Coquitlam, BC V3C 6K5 · 604-461-5602 · store.westernskybooks.com

Conferences and Events

SIWC at Sea 2020 · 29 March–25 April 2020 · siwc.ca/siwc-at-sea

Creative Ink Festival · 15–17 May 2020 Burnaby, BC · creativeinkfestival.com

When Words Collide · 14–16 August 2020 Calgary, AB · whenwordscollide.org

Surrey International Writers' Conference 23–25 October 2020 · Surrey, BC · siwc.ca

Do you have a **story to tell?**
We can help!

Dreamers is dedicated to heartfelt writing. Visit our site for:

• Therapeutic Writing

• Poems & Stories

• Content Marketing

• Creative Nonfiction

• Writing Workshops

• Contests & Anthologies

• Residencies & Retreats

• ...and so much more!

www.DreamersWriting.com

DREAMERS
CREATIVE WRITING

PULP
Literature
JJ Lee
'The Man In the
Long Black Coat

PULP
Literature
Carol Berg
'Uncanonical Murder'

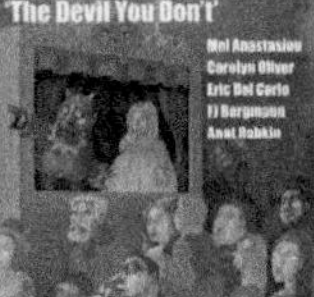
PULP
Literature
Matthew Hughes
'The Devil You Don't'
Mel Anastasiou
Carolyn Oliver
Eric Del Carlo
JJ Bergmann
Anat Rabkin
Allaigna's Song: Aria

PULP
Literature
George McWhirter
'Stalk'

Allaigna's Song
Overture
JM Landels

PULP
Literature

FANTASTIC
FRESH
FICTION

www.pulpliterature.com

The Digest Enthusiast
Book Ten
June 2019
Tom Brinkmann
Steve Carper
Peter Enfantino
Vince Nowell, Sr.
James Reasoner
Robert Snashall
Joe Wehrle, Jr.

MICHAEL KAMAKANA
ADVENT
WE THOUGHT WE KNEW WHAT THEY WANTED
WE WERE WRONG

Dear Geist...

I have been writing and rewriting a creative non-fiction story for about a year. How do I know when the story is ready to send out?

—*Teetering, Gimli MB*

Which is correct, 4:00, four o'clock or 1600 h?
—Floria, Windsor ON

Dear Geist,
In my fiction writing workshop, one person said I should write a lot more about the dad character. Another person said that the dad character is superfluous and I should delete him. Both of these writers are very astute. Help!

—Dave, Red Deer AB

Advice for the Lit-Lorn

Are you a writer?
Do you have a writing question, conundrum, dispute, dilemma, quandary or pickle?

Geist offers free professional advice to writers of fiction, non-fiction and everything in between, straight from Mary Schendlinger (Senior Editor of *Geist* for 25 years) and *Geist* editorial staff.

Send your question to advice@geist.com.

We will reply to all answerable questions, whether or not we post them.

geist.com/lit-lorn

GEIST
FACT · FICTION · NORTH of AMERICA

CONTESTS

Pulp Literature runs four annual contests for poetry, flash fiction, and short stories. For contest guidelines, prizes, and entry fees, see pulpliterature.com/contests.

The Bumblebee Flash Fiction Contest
Contest opens: 1 January 2020
Deadline: 15 February 2020
Winner notified: 15 March 2020
Winner published: Issue 27, Summer 2020
Prize: $300

The Magpie Award for Poetry
Contest opens: 1 March 2020
Deadline: 15 April 2020
Winner notified: 15 May 2020
Winner published: Issue 28, Autumn 2020
Prize: $500

The Hummingbird Flash Fiction Prize
Contest opens: 1 May 2020
Deadline: 15 June 2020
Winner notified: 15 July 2020
Winner published: Issue 29, Winter 2021
Prize: $300

The Raven Short Story Contest
Contest opens: 1 September 2020
Deadline: 15 October 2020
Winner notified: 15 November 2020
Winner published: Issue 26, Spring 2021
Prize: $300

$\mathcal{B}$ECOME A PATRON OF PULP LITERATURE

By supporting *Pulp Literature* on Patreon with $2 or more per month, you will be laying the foundation for a secure future for the magazine, as well as ensuring that you never miss an issue! Your subscription includes four big issues of short stories, novellas, poetry, comics, and novel excerpts, delivered to your door or electronic mailbox each year. **Find us at patreon.com/pulplit**

If you prefer to subscribe through our website, go to pulpliterature. com/subscribe.

Or you can send a cheque with the form below to
Subscriptions, Pulp Literature Press, 21955 16 Ave, Langley BC, V2Z 1K5, Canada

---

Don't miss an issue!

- ❏ **Send me 2 years (8 issues) at the special rate of $90** (save $30)*
- ❏ **Send me 1 year (4 issues) for $50** (save $10)*
- ❏ **Send me 2 years of digital issues for $30** (save $9.92)
- ❏ **Send me 1 year of digital issues for $17.50** (save $2.47)

Name: ____

Address: ____

City: ______________________________ Prov. / State: _________

Postal code: ______________ Country: __________________

Email: ____

- ❏ **Payment enclosed**
- ❏ **Bill me**
- ❏ **New**
- ❏ **Renewal**

Make cheques payable in Canadian funds to J. Landels. Include email address for digital editions and Paypal billing, or subscribe at www.pulpliterature.com.

*for postage outside Canada add $20 per year in North America or $36 per year overseas.

www.ingramcontent.com/pod-product-compliance
Lightning Source LLC
Chambersburg PA
CBHW061253210726

48293CB00003B/948